Praise for *Brother XII's Treasure*

"A charming yarn in the classic British kids' own tradition, sure to appeal to fans of *Swallows and Amazons* and *The Penderwicks*, replete with detail and paced in the sure knowledge that getting there is half the fun."

TED STAUNTON, author of *Who I'm Not* and *Jump Cut*

"Books with mystery + adventure + danger have always been my favourite kind of story. A sailing adventure where kids are the crew, *Brother XII's Treasure* delivers on all three! Part of the intrigue is that the story is based on a true villain. Add the hunt for buried treasure and it equals a perfect fast-paced read."

LINDA DEMEULEMEESTER, author of the Grim Hill series

"A good, old-fashioned adventure at sea, embellished with details of a fascinating and little-known corner of British Columbian history."

ROBERT PAUL WESTON, author of *The Creature Department* and *Zorgamazoo*

"More than a detective story of youthful sleuthing, *Brother XII's Treasure* is a treasure trove of sailing lore, natural history, and BC coastal geography. Amanda Spottiswoode's story is as charming and unpretentious as her young characters. Brimful with the resourcefulness and camaraderie of pre-teen brothers, sisters, and friends, the young characters share a magical, if mysterious and scary, summer. This is an enchanting and heart-warming tale in much the same spirit as Arthur Ransome's ageless *Swallows and Amazons*."

PETER JOHNSON, author of *To the Lighthouse: An Explorer's Guide to the Island Lighthouses of Southwestern* BC

BROTHER XII's TREASURE

AMANDA SPOTTISWOODE

with ILLUSTRATIONS *by* MOLLY MARCH

PAPL
DISCARDED

Victoria | Vancouver | Calgary

Heritage House Publishing Company Ltd.
heritagehouse.ca

Cataloguing information available from Library and Archives Canada
978-1-77203-071-6 (pbk)
978-1-77203-072-3 (epub)
978-1-77203-073-0 (epdf)

Edited by Lara Kordic
Proofread by Lesley Cameron
Interior book design by Setareh Ashrafologhalai
Cover and interior illustrations and maps by Molly March

The interior of this book was produced on 100%
post-consumer recycled paper, processed chlorine
free and printed with vegetable-based inks.

Heritage House acknowledges the financial support for its
publishing program from the Government of Canada through
the Canada Book Fund (CBF), Canada Council for the Arts, and
the Province of British Columbia through the British Columbia
Arts Council and the Book Publishing Tax Credit.

19 18 17 16 15   1 2 3 4 5

Printed in Canada

For Tomas

CONTENTS

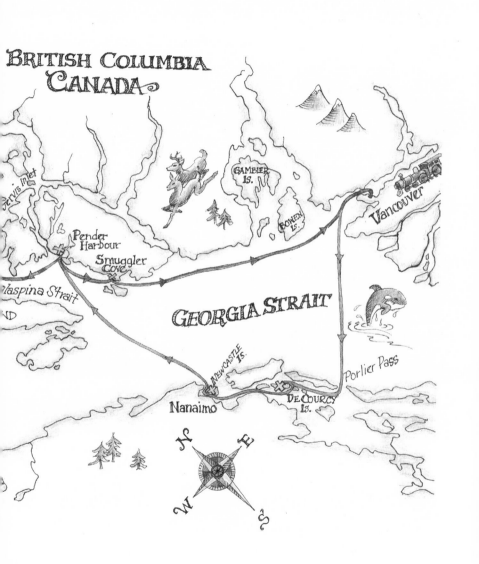

CHAPTER ONE

THE ADVENTURE BEGINS

Spring 1936

THE LETTERS ALL arrived on the same day—one to the boarding school in North Wales where Sophie, Harriet, and Posy were pupils; one to their brother, Ian, at his school in Devon; one to their friends Molly and Leticia at their home in Scotland; and the last to Molly and Leticia's brother, Mark, at his boarding school in Edinburgh.

Mail at the girls' boarding school was delivered at morning break time, known at the school as "elevenses," and Sophie and her sisters sat down with their bottles of milk and iced buns in great anticipation. It was clear the letter had come from Canada, and the only person they knew in Canada was Molly and Leticia's uncle Bert. Molly had written that he was currently holed up in a cabin somewhere on the west coast of Canada working on his current book—a history of the North-West Mounted Police, now known as the RCMP.

The children had met three summers ago, when the Phillips family was holidaying in Scotland. Their home was in the west of England, close to the naval base at Portsmouth, where their father, a commander in the Royal Navy, was stationed. He had been sent on assignment to the naval base on the River Clyde near Glasgow, and the rest of the family had rented a house in the village of Plockton, not far from the Isle of Skye on the west coast, close enough that Commander Phillips was able to visit every other weekend.

The village was on the edge of a sea loch, Loch Carron, and the children's father rented a sailing dinghy for them. There they met Molly and Leticia, and their brother, Mark, who lived across the loch with their widowed mother, Fiona Mac-Tavish, and her bachelor brother, Bert Cameron. The seven children became firm friends and spent the following two summers exploring the loch and surrounding hills and forests. They camped on one of the islands in the loch, raced their dinghy against the one owned by the MacTavish children, had mock battles, and searched for hidden treasure. Last summer Uncle Bert joined in their adventures by chartering a thirty-foot sloop and taking the entire crew of seven children on a cruise around the myriad islands off the Scottish coast. They spent splendid evenings anchored in snug coves, regaled by tales of Bert's round-the-world adventures. He had crewed on a tea clipper, climbed the foothills of the Himalayas, walked on the Great Wall of China, and panned for gold in Australia. Some of his stories were pretty far-fetched, but Fiona MacTavish had assured her children that most were true. Bert funded his addiction to international travel by writing guidebooks as well as books about famous historical characters and events. Officially he was Uncle Bert, but unofficially, to his nieces and nephew, and their friends, he was Captain Gunn.

SOPHIE OPENED THE letter, carefully saving the colourful stamp for Mark's stamp collection. Harriet and Posy waited with bated breath as Sophie smoothed the flimsy airmail paper and began to read:

Ahoy, fellow mariners and explorers!

Adventure beckons! My book is coming along well and I have given myself a holiday from my master and constant companion, the typewriter. I have chartered a yacht for the summer and think the time is right for us to explore the New World.

Therefore, instead of going home at the end of the summer term, you will proceed by train to Southampton via London, where the entire crew and your respective mothers will meet up. The admirals (mothers) will have brought your travel documents and luggage for the voyage, so don't worry about only having school clothes with you. At Southampton you will board the *Empress of Britain* and cross the Atlantic to Quebec City. From there you will catch a train to Montreal, from whence you will take the transcontinental train to Vancouver. I will meet you there.

I advise you to spend the time on-board ship researching the history of British Columbia (there is an excellent library on-board), focusing on possible hidden pirate treasure.

I look forward to meeting you when you arrive in Vancouver.

Yours truly,

UNCLE BERT, A.K.A. CAPTAIN GUNN

P.S. I appoint Sophie as Chief Commanding Officer in Charge of Explorers on the voyage, so do as she says! Those disobeying will be keelhauled on arrival!

Sophie's mind flew to what clothes their mother would pack for a sea voyage followed by intrepid exploring in an untamed land. Harriet immediately began to make a list of notebooks, paints, crayons, and other materials she would need as the official log keeper of all the children's expeditions. Posy was just thankful to be included in the upcoming adventure. As the youngest of all the children, and despite the fact that she was now eight years old, she was all too often referred to as the baby of the group.

THE REST OF the term dragged interminably. Letters flew back and forth between all the children, speculating about what kind of boat Captain Gunn would find for them, where they would go, and, most importantly, what adventures they would have once they set sail.

Sophie and her brother and sisters were thrilled to hear that their father, Commander Phillips, would meet them when the *Empress of Britain* berthed in Quebec City. He was in charge of HMS Hood, a warship currently serving with the Atlantic Fleet. The ship had been on a transatlantic exercise and would be docked in Montreal when the children arrived. He would escort them by train from Quebec to Montreal and see them safely on the train to Vancouver. The children hadn't seen him for several months, and this unexpected meeting added an extra dimension to the incredible adventure they were embarking on.

Harriet read up about the early history of western Canada and was astonished to find that European people had been settled there for less than a hundred years. Before the mid-1800s that part of the country had been totally inhabited by different Native tribes, whose culture and lifestyle fascinated her intensely.

"The problem will be what adventure to choose," she mused. "I think that finding an abandoned gold mine and discovering a new load of gold would be a great adventure. I've been reading about the gold rush, and I think we have a really good chance of finding gold in Canada. Even though the gold rush ended, they say that there are still masses to be found. It's just not quite as easy to strike it big as it was in the 1850s."

"I hope the boat Captain Gunn charters has a good galley," said Sophie. At nearly fourteen and the oldest girl in the group, she anticipated that meal preparation would be her responsibility for the most part. She couldn't imagine Captain Gunn was much use in the kitchen. The boys wouldn't think of helping, and the younger girls—with the exception of Leticia and

Harriet—would be more of a bother in the kitchen than a help. Still, she didn't mind cooking; she actually quite liked the lessons she'd received from the family's cook when she was last home from school. So as the trip drew near, Sophie began planning meals and wondering what sort of food she would find in the grocers' shops in Vancouver.

Meanwhile, Ian had been doing his own speculating about the upcoming trip. He scoured his school library for information about sailing on the west coast and discovered that there were literally thousands of small islands in between Vancouver Island and the mainland—perfect for exploring. He had also been reading up on the fearsome tidal rapids that dot the BC coast. Ian was in his last year at his current school. He was starting at the Royal Navy College at Dartmouth in the autumn. Ian planned to follow his father into the Royal Navy and knew that navigation was a key part of his upcoming education. His father had taught him to sail when he was very young in a small dinghy that they kept near their home in Devon. As well, he had had lots of practice sailing the rented fourteen-foot clinker-built dinghy on the Scottish loch and helping Captain Gunn on their cruise the previous summer. Here was a marvellous opportunity to practise his navigational skills on a remote and complicated coast. He was looking forward to navigating the maze of islands, rocks, tidal rapids, and other hazards they would encounter. His precious box containing his collection of marine instruments never left his possession and would be the only thing he would pack if he were limited to one item of baggage.

Mark had two thoughts: "I wonder what kind of engine the boat will have," quickly followed by: "I hope Uncle Bert hasn't forgotten that I'm the chief engineer on all our expeditions."

Although Mark could sail their dinghy just as well as his sisters could, his real passion was for engines. It didn't really matter whether the engine was in a car, a train, or a boat. He loved to tinker and was always on hand to help his uncle when he was fixing the family's car or the stately motor launch that had taken them on many an outing on the sea loch that bordered their home.

AT HOME ON that northern Scottish loch, Molly and Leticia bore the last few weeks at their day school with barely contained impatience. Their house overlooked the sea loch, and was called An Cuileann, which means "the holly" in Gaelic. It was separated from the road by a hedge of hollies, and the grounds swept down to the loch, where the family's dinghy was moored in the old boathouse.

"This is the very best adventure Uncle Bert has ever thought of," Molly said to her mother as they were packing their duffel bags in preparation for their departure to Southampton the next day.

"I just hope he doesn't get fed up with the lot of you after enjoying months of peace in his cabin," said Mrs. MacTavish. "You must promise to give him some time to relax. This is supposed to be a holiday for him. He'd have been better off booking a couple of weeks in the Bahamas without a gang of kids."

"What fun would that be?" asked Leticia as she folded shirts and shorts into her bag.

Molly watched in dismay as her mother brought several party frocks out of the wardrobe.

"We won't want those," she said. "We're going sailing, not to parties."

"You are lucky enough to have been given a wonderful trip on an ocean liner," responded her mother with a laugh. "Try and behave like young ladies, not the hooligans you really are! You will be expected to change for dinner on-board, and Sophie will be in charge of making sure you all show up looking respectable."

Molly sighed dramatically, but it was just for show. As the oldest of the MacTavish children (at thirteen and a half), she had felt a responsibility to her mother ever since her father died. Molly was just four years old when the accident happened—it was a snowy night in January when Mr. MacTavish lost control of his car and skidded off the road. Leticia was two years old at the time, and Fiona was still pregnant with Mark, so Molly was the only one of the three children who had any memory of their father and the effect his death had on their mother.

As a single parent, Mrs. MacTavish gave her children the freedom to explore the world around them and encouraged them in all their adventures. She and her brother, Bert, had lost their own parents at a very young age and had been brought up by a very straight-laced spinster aunt. Aunt Bertha still made occasional and unwelcome appearances at their home in Scotland, and it may have been as a reaction to that restrained and controlled upbringing that Fiona allowed her children unprecedented freedoms. She fully expected both Molly and Leticia to make their way in the world on an equal footing with men, and of course expected her young son to treat his sisters as equals. She'd lay her bets on Molly any day in a sailing race against the best male sailors of her age. For her part, Molly tried to live up to her mother's expectations, acting like the "girl who should have been a boy" in all their adventures, kitting herself and her brother and sister out as pirates. But she was growing up.

AT LONG LAST the final day of term arrived. Mrs. Phillips had arranged with Ian's school for him to leave a few days before the official end of term and arrive in Southampton at the same time as the others.

It was as if a piece of rope had become unravelled and was now being twisted back into one strand. Ian and his mother chugged their way eastwards from Devon, while the girls at school in North Wales had negotiated a change of trains in Crewe, where they were reunited with Mrs. MacTavish, Molly, Leticia, and Mark, who were travelling on the fast train from Glasgow. Mark had met up with the rest of his family at the station in Glasgow after travelling alone from his boarding school in Edinburgh. Mrs. Phillips and Ian would arrive at Paddington Station in London and then cross the city to meet the others at Euston Station, where trains from Scotland and the north of England terminated. They would all spend the night in a London hotel before catching the train to Southampton the next morning. It was a travel plan whose military precision would have impressed any admiral.

At the Crewe train station the MacTavish children greeted Sophie, Harriet, and Posy with whoops (from Molly) and hugs all around. Mrs. MacTavish's cook, Mrs. Baird, had packed a splendid picnic basket. As the official provider for countless expeditions she knew exactly what would get this expedition off to a good start. Mrs. MacTavish unpacked the hamper to reveal homemade sausage rolls, tomatoes from the greenhouse, apples that had been stored over the winter in the root cellar, grog (lemonade to landlubbers), and a tin of Mrs. Baird's best toffee. There was also a huge Thermos flask of tea. They settled in for the journey onwards to London and tucked into their feast.

"Bert told me in his last letter that he knows the captain of the *Empress of Britain*," said Mrs. MacTavish. "They met when they were both in Singapore—having a nice cool drink at Raffles, no doubt!"

Molly could sense that her mother was about to launch into a lecture.

"Don't forget that Sophie is Chief Commanding Officer in Charge of Explorers on-board, and you are to do what she says," Mrs. MacTavish continued. "Including, I might say, dressing properly for dinner. I don't want it to get back to Uncle Bert that his nieces and nephew and their friends were a pack of hooligans on-board!"

"Mother!" exclaimed Molly. "You know we can be perfect angels when we put our minds to it. Remember how we showed up for tea dressed like little ladies when Aunt Bertha was staying?"

"Yes," her mother replied, "and I also remember how you forgot to remove your red caps! Nice with shorts, not such a good look with a lace party frock!"

Molly fingered her striped cap with a rueful smile. It was the girls' trademark to wear red-and-white knitted caps, even in the warmest of weather. Mark, who felt he was more an engineer than a pirate, had acquired a train conductor's cap, which he wore whenever he thought he could get away with it. Molly had packed two caps each for her and Leticia, one in wool and one in cotton, in case it got hot.

"What's the weather like in Canada?" asked Harriet. "I'm afraid it might be freezing, and I really hope there aren't any polar bears."

Mrs. MacTavish sighed. An English private school education might be good for developing skills in English, science, and maths, but the curriculum was sadly lacking in the study of foreign countries, except where it pertained to the advancement of the British Empire. When they had touched on Canada in their geography lessons, the only two facts that had stuck in Harriet's mind—and this was a girl who had a mind like a sponge—was that Canada exported millions of matches and mined bauxite, used to make aluminum.

"I believe that summer on the west coast of Canada is about the same as summer here," she replied. "And as most of your cruise will be in August, I'm pretty sure you will get in lots of swimming and sunbathing. Bert tells me there are plenty of lakes you can get to, as well as swimming in the sea. Sophie, I'm sure you will make sure that Posy doesn't swim out of her depth."

Sophie was beginning to feel the responsibilities of the trip weighing her down a little. It was one thing to be the one in charge of wholesome meals, baths, and proper bedtimes, but she was also an adventurer like the rest of them. *Oh, well, she thought. It's a small price to pay for the incredible trip Captain Gunn has arranged for us.* She just hoped that shipboard life, free of parental presence, wouldn't go to their heads. Once they got to Vancouver, Captain Gunn would be in charge and she could relinquish her Commander-in-Chief title with relief.

After lunch, Mrs. MacTavish leaned back in her seat for a nap, and the others spent the rest of the trip reading and watching the green fields and small towns whiz by. Finally, the train slowed to a crawl and the fields gave way to grim tenements backing onto the railway line, with smutty washing stretched across the walled back gardens. Not for the first time, Sophie privately mused about the lives of the people who lived in these houses and how different they were from her idyllic life in the privileged atmosphere of a private school and her family's holidays in Scotland, not to mention a nice dollop of foreign travel.

The train finally pulled into Euston Station and with a last steamy exhale ground to a halt. Luggage was pulled off the racks and personal possessions gathered, and the seven of them descended onto the platform. As they exited the gates to the concourse, Molly gave a blood-curdling yell. Ian burst from the crowd, and the whole crew were reunited. Mrs. MacTavish greeted Mrs. Phillips with a kiss, and they collected all the luggage on a trolley and headed for the exit.

"I've got two taxis waiting to take us to the hotel," said Mrs. Phillips. "Time for a quick supper before early bed. We will have to get up early tomorrow to catch the train to Southampton."

The next morning, after a full English breakfast (eggs, bacon, sausages, tomatoes, mushrooms, fried bread, toast, marmalade, and gallons of tea), the crew and their respective mothers loaded everyone, along with the luggage, into two taxis. The cacophony of London traffic and the smell of exhaust fumes assailed them through the open windows. What a difference from the tranquility of Scotland, Wales, and Devon! The taxis inched their way through the traffic and onto Waterloo Bridge.

"Oh, look!" gasped Posy. "I can see Big Ben!"

Sure enough, Big Ben's tower rose majestically from the Houses of Parliament. The river passed below them with every kind of watercraft going up, down, and across the water. It looked like collisions were a certainty, but the boat operators were skilled, and the apparent chaos was in fact an orchestrated ballet of boats travelling along one of England's most ancient waterways.

A few minutes later they arrived at Waterloo Station and unloaded all the luggage onto a porter's trolley, before racing to catch the train to Southampton. Just as the last bag was heaved aboard and the last of the crew were jumping into the carriage, the whistle blew and the train began gathering speed.

"And we haven't even left England yet," said Harriet as she flopped into one of the window seats. "I've been studying my atlas, and it's almost six thousand miles from England to Vancouver. I feel as if I've travelled half of that already!"

"Don't worry," said Mrs. Phillips. "You'll have plenty of time to relax on the ship."

"I don't think so," replied Harriet. "Captain Gunn has given us lots of homework. My job is to research the ship's library for possible buried treasure sites in Canada, and Ian is supposed to brush up on his navigation skills. We're going exploring in uncharted waters!"

"Well, make sure you leave time for some fun," said Mrs. MacTavish. "But not too much fun," she added hastily as she caught the gleam in Molly's eye.

The journey to Southampton only took an hour and a half. At the station they found a bus waiting to collect all the passengers off the London train who were bound for the docks and the *Empress of Britain*.

As they passed through the dock gates and along the massive quay dotted with crates, cranes, trolleys, and carts and buzzing with stevedores, porters, and passengers, the entire crew gasped and fell silent. Even Molly was momentarily struck dumb!

The *Empress of Britain* rose massively and majestically from her berth at the quay. She was over three hundred feet long and a hundred feet wide, and her three huge funnels topped row upon row of portholes, decks, lifeboats, and rigging.

"I bet there's lots of places to explore," Mark finally piped up.

Mrs. MacTavish and Mrs. Phillips glanced at each other. The reality was beginning to set in—they were sending their children halfway around the world, and who knew what sorts of adventures Bert Cameron was cooking up for them in his west coast cabin?

And then the moment passed. The children began chattering excitedly again, and the mothers gave each other a wan smile. They had brought up a crew of remarkably responsible children and knew that with Sophie in charge on-board, and with the considerable (if sometimes misused) intelligence of Molly and Ian, all would be fine. The children would also be in the charge of a steward and stewardess assigned to their three cabins—all arranged in advance by Uncle Bert, a.k.a. Captain Gunn.

SEVERAL HOURS LATER, travel documents examined, ship boarded via the gangplank that hung between ship and shore, and cabins inspected by the mothers, it was time for all friends and family not actually travelling to go ashore. Many hugs and a few tears later, Mrs. MacTavish and Mrs. Phillips descended the gangplank and stood on the quay with the crowd waiting to watch the great ship departing.

"Give your father a big hug from me," Mrs. Phillips had called.

"And the same to Uncle Bert from me," added Mrs. MacTavish. "And tell him we're shipping him seven children, and I expect to get the same number home again!"

With a loud blast of the whistle, the massive mooring lines were slipped from the capstans and the four tugs eased the ship away from her berth.

The children lined the rail far above and waved and yelled until the fluttering handkerchiefs of the mothers were tiny specks of white.

"We're off at last," said Molly. "Now the adventure begins. Three cheers!"

CHAPTER TWO
THE NEW WORLD

THE CREW CRAMMED into one cabin for a powwow. Sophie, Harriet, and Posy were in one cabin, with bunk beds for the two older girls and a pull-out bed for Posy. Molly and Leticia shared the cabin next door. A door from each cabin led into a shared bathroom. Everything was neat and shipshape. There were built-in cupboards, drawers, and a wardrobe in each cabin. The mothers had supervised the unpacking, and everything was neatly stowed. The two boys had a cabin a little farther along the passageway and shared a bathroom with another cabin. Now they arranged themselves on the bunks and in the one easy chair in the Phillips girls' cabin. Harriet was appointed official minute taker of all explorers' meetings and had her notebook ready.

"We need to make sure we are on time for all meals," started Sophie, "and everyone must be washed, hair brushed, and dressed appropriately."

Mark and Molly rolled their eyes but quickly nodded in agreement when they caught a stern look from Ian. As the oldest of the whole gang, he felt some responsibility for their behaviour, though he mostly left it up to Sophie to keep the little ones in line.

"There are lots of things to do on-board," he said. "Look, here's a schedule of activities." He picked up a pamphlet from the small table. "There's a costume ball on the fourth night at sea and lectures every day. There's a talk about the Native culture of North America and another about the gold rush in western Canada."

"I'm not going to lectures," piped up Mark. "I had enough of lecturing at school. I want to explore the ship and maybe see the engine room."

"I'm pretty sure the engine room is off limits to passengers, especially small boys," said Sophie.

"I think that apart from meals, we should all do what interests us," said Molly. "We're all going to be together on Captain Gunn's ship when we get there, so we don't all need to stay in a group for the next five days."

Sophie was sensing mutiny, and they'd only been on-board for a few hours.

"How about we meet at meals and have a check just before dinner to make sure everyone is accounted for? Obviously Posy stays with me at all times," she said.

There was a knock on the door and the door opened to reveal a young man dressed in a spotless starched white uniform.

"Hello, I'm Michel, your steward for the voyage," he said in a charming French accent. "Your stewardess is Bettine, and she'll be along to introduce herself later. I've brought you an invitation to dinner at the captain's table tonight—quite an honour as normally you would be dining in the second-class dining room."

"I bet Captain Gunn arranged that," said Molly. "I suppose it's just as well that Mother made us pack our 'pretties.'"

THAT AFTERNOON, ONCE they had cleared the Solent and were heading down the English Channel towards the open Atlantic, the alarm bells positioned around the ship started clanging simultaneously. The loudspeaker outside the children's cabins broadcast the following message: "Lifeboat drill, lifeboat drill. Proceed to your muster stations immediately with your life jackets."

Everyone grabbed their life jackets from under the bunks and headed up on deck.

"Listen carefully and pay attention," said Sophie. "Remember that even ocean liners designed to be unsinkable can still sink."

Posy looked scared, so Sophie hastily added, "Of course, we're not going to sink. It's only a formality, but we need to be prepared just in case."

The crew demonstrated the lowering of the lifeboats and showed everyone how to board them. It didn't take very long, and soon everyone was allowed to return to their cabins. Molly secretly thought it would be tremendous fun if the ship sank and they all had to take to the lifeboats, but she wisely kept this thought to herself.

A couple of hours later, all washed and dressed for dinner in the first-class dining room, the crew presented themselves to the formidable maître d' at the entrance to the grand room. They had pulled out the very best of their dressy clothes for the occasion, and the girls were outfitted in pretty party frocks, white socks, and black patent leather shoes. Molly had even tied a blue ribbon around her head (not a red cap to be seen), and the other girls' hair was neatly plaited. The boys were in dress shorts, clean white shirts, and ties. The maître d' steered them through the tables, set with gleaming white cloths and crystal glasses. A string quartet played quietly in one corner, and the other passengers were milling around looking for their places, dressed to the nines in evening gowns and full dinner suits. The room itself was magnificent, with panelled walls of inlaid wood, marble pillars, and floors covered with thick, colourful carpets with intricate designs of flowers and birds woven into them.

The children were awestruck by the opulent surroundings. Molly kept swivelling around, not sure which detail to take in first, and bumping into Harriet, who was right behind her. Sophie took charge. She gave the entire crew a stern look and motioned for them to keep following their grand guide in an orderly fashion as he proceeded to the head table, where the captain was waiting for them. It was fortunate, Sophie thought, that they had all been receiving etiquette lessons their whole lives and knew how to behave in most social situations. But even she felt a twinge of fear as she took in the imposing figure at their table.

The captain was an impressive character, with iron-grey hair and a neatly trimmed beard and moustache. He was attired in full dress uniform—white trousers and jacket liberally adorned with gold braid and massive epaulettes on the shoulders. And if the uniform wasn't enough of a clue about who was in charge around here, his serious, steadfast expression left no doubt about his ability to guide his ship and its hundreds of passengers safely to their destination. Suddenly his stern gaze over the room melted into a smile as he spotted the approaching children.

"Welcome!" he boomed, rising from his seat to display his considerable height. "Any friend of Bert Cameron is a friend of mine—or should I say seven friends of mine! I'm Captain Blenkinsopp, and you are?"

The children quickly rearranged themselves into a line, more or less in order of height from tallest to shortest, and began formally—if somewhat awkwardly—introducing themselves to the captain. They were a little tongue-tied, and very aware of the other diners in the room, who were looking at them curiously and wondering who this gang of children was and why they had the privilege of being seated at the captain's table. After the introductions were over, there was a moment of silence as the children remained standing around the table, unsure of what to do. From their years of training at home and at school they knew it was impolite for children to speak until spoken to, and they were afraid to take their seats until the captain ordered them to. Finally, Mark broke the ice.

"I bet Uncle Bert wishes he could be here now—he loves food!"

The others held their breath, wondering how Mark's comment would be received.

To everyone's relief, Captain Blenkinsopp gave a huge guffaw, ruffled Mark's hair with his huge bear paw of a hand, and sat down unceremoniously on his chair. The others took that as a cue to do the same, and soon they were all chatting and laughing like old friends.

"Wish I was off on a west coast cruise," Captain Blenkinsopp said. "Trust old Bert to think up such a great adventure. We had some adventures of our own when we were in the Far East together."

Dinner progressed course by delicious course. *At least those private schools have taught us all good table manners*, thought Sophie. Captain Blenkinsopp asked them what they planned to do during the five-day transatlantic voyage.

"I'd love to see the engine room," said Mark, prompting a sharp kick under the table from Ian.

"Of course," replied the Captain. "I'll arrange it for you. And I think you, Ian, are heading off to Dartmouth College in the autumn. How would you like to spend some time with me on the bridge? You can navigate us across the Atlantic!"

Ian turned several shades of red and stammered his thanks. What an experience he was going to have! How many of his fellow new cadets would have been on the bridge of a great ship like this?

THE NEXT FIVE days passed in a whirl of games, explorations, and studies interspersed with delicious meals. The children had been brought up on good plain English food, and although they had occasionally been guests in houses where the food was prepared by a real chef rather than a cook, the meals on the *Empress of Britain* were like nothing they had ever tasted before. Breakfasts were served as a buffet that went way beyond the full English breakfast they enjoyed on Sundays at home. In addition to the usual bacon, sausage, mushrooms, and tomatoes, there were eggs done three ways, toast, croissants (no one had ever seen one of those before), fruit, porridge, and a selection of juices and hot beverages. And that was just breakfast.

Lunch and dinner were served sitting down in the second-class dining room (not as grand as the first-class dining room, but still pretty splendid). Lunch was usually soup followed by a main course and a pudding, but dinner was at least five courses. And in between lunch and dinner, they could take afternoon tea in one of the lounges. It was a good job that no one was on a diet!

Mark spent most of his time between meals following Bill, one of the junior engineers, as he worked on the four huge steam turbine engines that filled the engine room with their massive bulk, plus miles of piping, dials, levers, and gauges. Bill even let Mark help him polish and sweep the engine room to keep it spotless.

It remains a bit of a mystery what Molly and Leticia got up to during the voyage, but by the end they could have given guided tours into every nook and cranny of the ship they could get to. As well, they were occasionally seen engaged in energetic games of quoits and racing each other along the long, wide decks.

Ian was given the freedom to visit the bridge whenever he wanted. He mostly sat quietly in a corner, observing all the business of guiding the great ship safely across the Atlantic Ocean. He was even occasionally invited to take the helm, with the helmsman standing beside him, and made several minor course changes on the orders of the captain. He would certainly have some stories to tell when he started at Dartmouth—if his fellow cadets believed him!

Sophie enjoyed the trip the least. Her days were consumed with keeping Posy occupied, and she spent a lot of her time in the playroom with her youngest sister and other small children, playing games and taking trips outside to walk the decks and get a dose of fresh sea air.

Harriet befriended the ship's librarian. As Uncle Bert had promised, the library was exceptionally well appointed. The walls were lined with floor-to-ceiling bookshelves. There must have been thousands of books covering every subject under the sun, and many of them were leather-bound with gold-tooled spines. The librarian, seated at her desk beside boxes of card files, could retrieve any request in a matter of minutes. The room was furnished with tables and chairs for the readers who wanted to make notes, as well as comfortable chairs, upholstered in soft leather, set next to portholes overlooking the ocean. Harriet was, of course, focused on the history of the west coast of Canada, and the librarian, Mrs. Dickens, pulled out a stack of books on the subject for her to study. It wasn't often that one of the passengers spent so much time in her library, and she was happy to help the keen young researcher. Harriet pored over the stack of books, and on the fourth day at sea she hit pay dirt!

That evening, as the crew met before dinner, Harriet could hardly contain herself. It was the evening of the costume ball. The children had scoured the costume chests made available to passengers and were busy kitting themselves out. Posy was dressed as a fairy princess (the only costume she would consider wearing); Ian had found a small officer's uniform that made him look like one of the crew; Mark was dressed as a train engineer, complete with striped coveralls and a whistle (which Sophie forbade him to use); Molly and Leticia went as themselves—that is, pirates—in shorts and red-and-white caps, and with cardboard daggers shoved in their belts. Harriet went as an artist, in flowing draperies and a fantastic hat, and with a paintbrush between her teeth. That left Sophie, who was at a loss for inspiration until she found a beautiful embroidered gown, which, with the addition of a pointed hat and veil, turned her into a medieval queen. They made quite an impressive and eclectic group.

Finally everyone was dressed and ready, and they settled themselves around the bunks and chair in Molly and Leticia's cabin. Harriet took advantage of the momentary hush before everyone headed for the door to announce her find.

"I know what we're going to do as our adventure!" she exclaimed, jumping up in a whirl of draperies and dropping her paintbrush, which rolled under the bunk. "There really *is* buried treasure on the coast."

"What do you mean?" asked Leticia, scrambling out from under the bunk and wielding the missing paintbrush.

"There was someone called Brother xii who collected masses of gold and then disappeared with it," continued Harriet. "He lived on an island called De Courcy with a wicked woman named Madame Z and cheated loads of people out of all their worldly possessions. We're going to pass right by his island on our cruise—I've checked the map."

"That's amazing!" exclaimed Molly leaping to her feet and wielding her dagger. "What a perfect adventure for pirates and explorers! Do you know anything else?"

"The librarian is going to dig out a few more books, but really no one knows what happened to Brother xii and the gold. The police were after him because of the fraud and because there were reports that he'd been beating people, but someone must have warned him, because when the police arrived he'd vanished. They found a cellar where they think he hid the gold, and he left a note saying no one would ever track him down."

"He obviously never met us," laughed Molly. "We'll track him down and find the gold. This is going to be the best adventure ever!"

The prospect of an adventure involving a villain and a cache of buried treasure was just what the crew needed. For them, it wasn't enough to just go for a cruise. There had to be some purpose—and now they had it! The children headed to the big ballroom in high spirits. As they mingled with the other passengers, all decked out in a variety of fantastic costumes, they felt like the luckiest people aboard. Mark certainly felt lucky when he scanned the buffet tables groaning under a fabulous selection of hot and cold dishes. The centrepiece was an enormous ice sculpture of the *Empress* riding the icy waves.

Sophie allowed everyone to stay up until 10:00 p.m., way past their usual bedtime, and then firmly escorted them down to their cabins.

"The ship docks tomorrow, and we have to pack first thing in the morning," she reminded everyone, adding, "I can't wait to see Daddy!"

Molly, Mark, and Leticia always felt a little left out when the Phillips children talked about their father. Although Molly had some faint memories of her father, Leticia didn't remember him at all, and Mark wasn't even born at the time of his father's death. Of course, they had Uncle Bert, but sometimes they would have liked to have a father like Commander Phillips. Uncle Bert was great for cooking up adventures, but he could be a little unreliable and had a tendency to disappear into remote corners of the globe for months at a time.

Molly grabbed Leticia and signalled her to let the others go into their cabins first, then gestured to her sister to follow her up the companionway and out on deck. The moon cast a silvery glow on the calm water, and they could see that they had already left the open ocean and were heading into the Gulf of St. Lawrence. Molly grasped the rail and gazed in awe at the approaching coastline.

"The New World," she breathed. "We're just like those explorers who didn't know where they were going or what they were going to see. Anything could happen!"

"We'd better get back into our cabins before Sophie discovers we've gone," said Leticia. "We don't want any bad reports when she hands us over to Captain Gunn!"

"All right, all right," laughed Molly. "I'll be a goody two-shoes for another few days, and then—watch out, pirates and villains! Captain Molly, Pirate and Terror of the Seas, is coming to get you!"

THE NEXT MORNING the great ship was nudged into her dock by a team of tugs, and after the huge mooring lines were secured and the gangplank lowered, the children queued up with the other passengers to disembark.

As they finally reached the top of the gangplank and could see over the other departing passengers, Sophie's usually calm demeanour left her and she yelled at the top of her voice.

"Daddy, Daddy, we're here!"

A tall, distinguished-looking man in a Royal Navy uniform had been allowed past the barriers holding back other members of the public meeting passengers off the ship. He met them at the foot of the gangplank, and his children greeted him with hugs and kisses. Only Ian held back and was given a warm handshake and brief hug from his father after the others had let him go. The MacTavish children were duly greeted too, and then the whole crew headed for Immigration and Customs. From there, they quickly reclaimed their baggage, and Commander Phillips ushered them out of the dock area and into two waiting taxis.

"Not much time to lose," he said as he settled back into the first taxi with Harriet and Posy clinging to his arms. "The train to Montreal leaves in an hour."

It was a twenty-minute drive from the port to the railway station, and the route took them along the great St. Lawrence River, which seemed to have almost as much boat traffic as the River Thames. There was so much to see but no time to see it.

"I would have liked to take you all on a tour of old Quebec City, but the train times just wouldn't allow it. Oh well. I'm sure you are keen to get on with the next leg of your trip. Another four days cooped up on a train, with a lot less room to run around than on-board ship. Mark, I want you to leave the driving of the train to the engineer! I'll bet Bert Cameron is relieved that he's not making this leg of the journey with you! In any case, it will be a great opportunity to see the size of this country. Did you know that after crossing the ocean you are still only halfway to Vancouver?"

After a relatively short train journey from Quebec City to Montreal, during which the four Phillips children caught up on all the news from their father and he quizzed them on how they were all doing at school as well as how their mother had been when they had said goodbye to her five days earlier, the train pulled into Montreal's impressive railway station. A porter helped transport all their luggage to a different platform, where the transcontinental train with "Vancouver" displayed on its destination board was waiting for them. Mark noted that trains in Canada were visible from the rails up, rather than just the upper part of the train as seen in England, where the high platforms cut the view of the train off at the level of the passenger doors. The smartly dressed rail attendants checked their tickets and helped them aboard via the portable steps positioned at each door. The children were assigned seats in a long compartment, and the attendant showed them how the seats turned into bunks at night with thick wool curtains to shut them in from the rest of the passengers.

All too soon it was time to say goodbye to Commander Phillips. Harriet and Posy were in tears, but their father comforted them. "You are having the most incredible adventure, and I expect to hear all about it at Christmas." Harriet's face lit up. "Oh, didn't I tell you? My ship will be back in Portsmouth at the end of November, and your mother and I are making plans for a Christmas holiday in Scotland. Mrs. MacTavish has invited us all to stay."

All the children were thrilled by this news, and Harriet and Posy dried their tears as they all started chattering about the prospect of yet more adventures. All too soon, the stationmaster was walking up and down the platform shouting,

"Anybody not travelling, please disembark. The train is leaving in five minutes."

The children said goodbye to Commander Phillips, who dispensed hugs all round. "Give my commiserations to poor Bert Cameron," he said with a laugh. "Although I suppose he's used to the hijinks of you MacTavishes! Try and give him some time off to relax. Poor chap doesn't know what he's taking on!"

In fact, Captain Gunn knew exactly what he was taking on. He'd been involved in adventures and pirating with his nieces, nephew, and the Phillips children before. Still, Commander Phillips hoped that Captain Gunn would use the next four days to rest up as the children sped their way across Canada. It was clear that once the children arrived in Vancouver, the poor old chap would be getting very little rest!

FOUR AND A HALF days later, the train was finally approaching the end of the line in Vancouver. The trip had been uneventful, with the children rotating between their seats, the dining car, and the observation car at the end of the train. The trip across the prairies had seemed endless. They could hardly believe that a country could be so vast and flat, that is until the Rocky Mountains appeared and then they could hardly believe that the train could find a way through them. The journey through the Rockies rendered even Mark speechless as massive peaks speared the cloudless blue sky and the train crossed and re-crossed canyons and roaring rivers. Finally the mountains flattened out as they approached the terminus in Vancouver.

The journey was almost at an end, and the adventure—which had begun what seemed like ages ago on the other side of the Atlantic—was about to enter a new phase. They couldn't wait to see Captain Gunn and tell him all about Brother XII and his hidden treasure. In their minds, finding it was only a matter of looking!

CHAPTER THREE
SETTING SAIL

THE CHILDREN CROWDED together at the window, craning their necks for the first glimpse of Captain Gunn. The train had been crawling through the Vancouver suburbs, and for the last little while they had been travelling beside the water with tantalizing glimpses of ships plying the waters of Burrard Inlet. Harriet had been studying her maps and knew that this particular bit of water was an inlet that wound its way deep into the coastline.

"There he is!" yelled Molly, dancing and jumping up and down as the train finally pulled into the Canadian Pacific Railway station on the city's downtown waterfront. "Quick, quick! Grab everything so we can be the first off the train."

The children quickly gathered all their hand baggage. Their big duffel bags were already packed and had been put in the luggage car ready to be offloaded by the porters. As the train sighed itself to a full stop, Molly flung open the door and leapt onto the platform before the porter had had time to position the steps.

She flew down the platform and flung herself at a stout middle-aged gentleman who was strolling towards them.

Captain Gunn was a rather odd figure among the respectably dressed passengers and railway staff. He wore a pair of baggy flannel trousers, kept more or less at waist level by a pair of suspenders. His shirt was open at the neck, exposing a loudly patterned scarf instead of a tie. His bald head was crowned by a straw panama hat adorned with a large feather tucked into the hatband. His feet were pushed into leather sandals.

"Well, well. So you made it," he said by way of greeting. "Hope you didn't lose anyone along the way." Captain Gunn cast his eyes over the remaining crewmembers, who had waited politely for the porter to help them down and were just now approaching along the platform.

It was hard to believe they had actually made it halfway around the world and were now chatting with Captain Gunn, last seen hauling up the anchor of a rented sailboat in Scotland the previous summer and sailing away to return it to its owner. He loved his sister and nieces and nephew, but preferred to live an independent and eccentric life, turning up unexpectedly every so often at his sister's house, where he holed up in his incredibly messy study, and then departing with very little notice for one of his frequent trips to remote corners of the world.

"I've asked the porters to cart your luggage along to the boat," said Captain Gunn as he headed for the exit with a niece hanging onto each arm and Mark trotting behind. "It's not far, and I thought you might like to stretch your legs after so many days cooped up."

They all trooped out of the station and were immediately engulfed in myriad street noises. Newspaper boys yelled out headlines as they hawked their papers, horses and carts clip-clopped over the cobblestones, motorcars blared their horns, and people hurried in all directions, dodging vehicles and horses as they crossed the street. It was overwhelming after their long voyage by ship and train, which had isolated them from the outside world. Never big fans of cities, the children looked forward to seeing the boat Captain Gunn had chartered and setting sail on their adventure.

"Hey, Uncle Bert!" yelled Molly over the noise. "Harriet's found us the perfect adventure! Just you wait; it's got everything! Villains, gold, islands—I can't wait to get going!"

"You can tell me all about it at dinner," replied Captain Gunn. "We're going to see the boat and then we're going for a slap-up Chinese dinner before we set sail in the morning."

After a fifteen-minute walk, they turned right down an alley and the water opened up before them. A forest of masts rose from the maze of docks that jutted out from the shore. They followed Captain Gunn as he negotiated a path along the wooden planked dock, with boats moored to left and right. What would their boat be like? Ian noticed several he would be happy to sail on, but Captain Gunn kept going. Finally, at the very end of the dock, he stopped.

"Here she is," he beamed. "A forty-one-foot schooner named South Islander. She's sailed across the Pacific from New Zealand. Her owner built her down there and named her after his island home. He's gone back there for a few months to visit his mother, and I've chartered her for our cruise."

The boat was beautiful. She had a gleaming white cabin roof and topsides with a smart green line below the gunwales, teak decks, lots of varnished woodwork, a roomy cockpit with bright cushions, and a long sleek cabin with brass portholes. The two masts raked slightly towards the stern, and there was a splendid bowsprit that Mark eyed with glee. What a place to climb out on and watch the sea swing by below!

"Welcome aboard!" called Captain Gunn as he hopped nimbly from the dock to the deck. "Gaff rigged with over a thousand square feet of sail. Draws nearly seven feet. She can do almost nine knots under full sail."

The children jumped aboard and did a circuit of the deck, noticing the skylight through which they could spy the cabin below, the masses of lines and rigging, and the neatly furled sails just waiting to spread their wings and carry them away from the city and into the greatest adventure of their lives. It was a boat that spoke to all of them.

"Look!" shouted Leticia from the side of the boat away from the dock. "There's a dinghy that looks just like ours at home!"

And indeed there was. Tied up alongside *South Islander*, with rope and tire fenders to protect them both, was a fourteen-foot clinker-built dinghy with its mast and spar rolled up in a sail along with a pair of oars.

"Came with the boat," said Captain Gunn. "That New Zealand chappie knew a thing or two about boat building. Built the dinghy alongside the big boat. Lived in the boat shed for three years while he was building them both. Too bad I couldn't rustle up another one—you'll just have to take turns. Now come below and I'll show you around. There's room for two in the forepeak, and there are two pilot berths aft. The saloon seats turn into another bed at night. I'm going to sleep in the cockpit. Very comfortable under an awning on those cushions. You can decide who sleeps where."

The children followed Captain Gunn through the companionway and down the steps into the cabin. There was a well-equipped galley; a navigation station; a tiny wood stove with tile surround; and a head with basin, shower, and toilet. All was spotless, and the settees were upholstered in gaily patterned material. There were lockers and cupboards everywhere, and Sophie paid particular attention to the galley with its oil-fired cookstove, two-burner stove top, and deep ice chest.

"We'll have to go shopping before we leave tomorrow," said Captain Gunn, noticing Sophie's interest in the cooking equipment. "I've had a sack of potatoes another of onions already delivered, but the rest we can get at my good friend Wei Chen's shop in Chinatown, where we're going for dinner tonight. He also owns a laundry, so we can get all our washing done tonight, and it will be delivered back to the boat in the morning."

A couple of hours later, after the porter from the train station had trundled their luggage along the dock, and everything had been neatly stowed, the crew headed out for Chinatown, with Ian and Mark carrying between them one of the duffel bags crammed with laundry. They walked eastwards from their dock in Coal Harbour and were soon in bustling Chinatown.

The crew were not strangers to the Chinese culture, having listened to Captain Gunn's tales of his travels to the East. He had even prepared them a couple of Chinese-style dinners, which they had greatly enjoyed. So it was with anticipation that Captain Gunn led them into a large restaurant furnished with long wooden tables and filled with chattering families enjoying dinner. They seated themselves at one of the tables and were immediately attended to by an elderly Chinese gentleman, elegantly robed, with a long pigtail hanging down his back.

"These are my crew," said Captain Gunn. "And, crew, this is Mr. Chen, a very good friend of mine."

Mr. Chen bowed and welcomed them, before snapping his fingers to summon one of the waiters.

"My nephew will bring you a delicious dinner for eight," he said. "Best Chinese food this side of Peking."

And indeed it was. While they tucked into the dishes with the chopsticks, which Captain Gunn had taught them to use for his forays into Chinese cuisine, he told them about Wei Chen's history.

"Been in North America for almost fifty years," he began. "Started in San Francisco during the gold rush and has done a bit of everything. Gold mining, building railways, shopkeeping, and any other business you could mention. Was given a pretty hard time of it in the early days, but he persevered and is now one of the richest men in Vancouver. Brought lots of his relatives over from China too. Very community-minded is Mr. Chen. Looks out for those who haven't been as lucky as him. Anyway, we'll go to his shop after dinner and stock up, and then everything, including the laundry, will be delivered to the boat in the morning. Now, tell me all about this adventure you have planned."

Everyone started to speak at once, but finally Captain Gunn made himself heard above the babble and asked Harriet to tell him the story.

"Well, to make a long story short, he was an Englishman who ended up in British Columbia leading a cult," began Harriet.

"What's a cult?" piped up Posy.

"Well, when I first found him in a book in the ship's library, I wondered the same thing, so I looked it up in the dictionary. It means 'a relatively small group of people having religious beliefs or practices regarded by others as strange or sinister.'"

The others exchanged amused glances. One of Harriet's many talents was looking things up in the dictionary and memorizing the definitions word for word. Once she had a word memorized, she never forgot it. Her mind was like a steel trap.

"And that's what he set himself up to be," Harriet continued. "A weird sort of religious leader. He managed to con quite a few people into joining him, and they had to hand over all their money as well. Anyway, they ended up living on De Courcy Island, which is one of the Gulf Islands between Victoria and Nanaimo. I know because they had a set of charts of the west coast on-board and I looked it up."

"Tell us again about the treasure," demanded Molly, who was at that moment picturing herself planting a pirate flag on top of a mountain of gold coins.

"Eventually, the police got involved and Brother xii disappeared with all the money he had collected from his followers," said Harriet. "He's never been seen since. Lots of people have looked for him and the treasure, but no one has had any luck. He just seemed to vanish into thin air."

"Sounds like a real villain, this Brother xii chap," Captain Gunn said, "and I think De Courcy Island would be a good place to start our search for the treasure. We can cross over Georgia Strait tomorrow, nip through Porlier Pass with the tide, and make De Courcy our first stop."

The dishes kept coming. The children recognized some—such as chow mein, sweet-and-sour pork, and chop suey—from Uncle Bert's experiments with Asian cooking. But there were also dishes that looked and tasted completely foreign. One that caused a bit of concern looked like—and in fact was—the tentacles of an octopus, but everyone was adventurous and tasted everything put on the table, declaring most of the dishes delicious. Eventually even Mark was full and the crew rolled out of the restaurant feeling very well fed indeed. During dinner Sophie had compiled a list of groceries, helped by suggestions from everyone. ("Don't forget the chocolate" was Mark's predictable contribution to the list, and Captain Gunn made sure to add pipe tobacco and a bottle of whisky.) Wei Chen's grocery store was a block away, and they all trooped in to the cavernous space, which was crowded from floor to ceiling with shelves containing some very odd-looking things in jars, sacks of rice, and towers of tins propped up around the floor. There was a potbellied stove in the middle of the store, and several Chinese men sat around smoking and playing checkers.

Wei Chen appeared from the back and, with the help of two more of his relatives, helped pile the supplies on the long wooden counter: tins of pemmican (corned beef to non-explorers), a large bag of rice and another of flour, tins of various vegetables, jars of marmalade, a box of slightly wizened apples, a wooden box of tea, a paper sack of sugar, several large tins of biscuits, and a large jar of cocoa. On and on it went, and the pile grew very large indeed.

"We won't be able to get fresh milk very often, so we'll take lots of tins of the evaporated stuff," said Captain Gunn. "And Wei Chen has some frozen meat for us in the back. We'll put it in the ice chest along with a couple of blocks of ice, and that should keep the fresh stuff good for quite a while. Mr. Chen has a big farm out in the valley, and he will deliver some fresh vegetables tomorrow along with the rest of this stuff. Oh, look here, we'll take some real pemmican. Great stuff made from dried moose meat and cranberries. All the proper explorers lived off it."

Last but definitely not least, there were a dozen large blocks of Mark's favourite milk chocolate.

"That's rationed," said Sophie, "or it will all disappear in a few days if Mark is allowed to eat it whenever he wants. Four squares each after dinner."

Once the selection of supplies was complete, Captain Gunn produced an enormous wad of cash from his bulging wallet, peeled off what looked like hundreds of dollar bills, and handed them to Mr. Chen, who bowed graciously and thanked them for their considerable business.

After a seemingly endless walk back to the boat, all the children tucked themselves into their bunks, while Captain Gunn bedded down in the cockpit.

"Goodnight, everyone," Leticia called into the darkness. "Our biggest adventure ever starts tomorrow."

"I think it's well and truly started," piped up Sophie. "Even if we had to turn round and start home tomorrow, I'd think we'd already had a tremendous adventure."

"Thank goodness we don't," said Molly. "Here we are, on the trail of real pirate gold. It doesn't get much better than that!"

"Go to sleep, all of you," came Captain Gunn's voice from the cockpit. "You have a busy day tomorrow learning the ropes."

Finally, peace descended on *South Islander*, broken only by the soft snores of Captain Gunn and the gentle slap of water against the hull.

THE NEXT MORNING the crew was up early getting the boat ready to leave when one of Mr. Chen's relatives arrived, trundling a cart filled with all their groceries and clean laundry. Sophie busied herself stowing all the food, including several large blocks of ice that went into the icebox along with packets of frozen meat. On a wooden grid on top of the ice and meat she was able to put all the perishable items, including a huge slab of cheese, several pounds of butter, some fresh vegetables, fresh milk in glass bottles (they would have the tins of evaporated to fall back on), bacon, sausages, and eggs. The crew was clearly not going to starve!

Meanwhile, Captain Gunn was going over the rigging and all the lines with the rest of the crew and briefing them on setting sail. He gave Mark a tour of the engine room (really just a cubby hole under the companionway) and a bag of rags and an oilcan.

Finally, they were ready to leave.

"We'll have to move over to the fuel dock to fill up with diesel and water," said Captain Gunn. "Drinking water is in the big barrel on the foredeck, but we have to fill the tanks for washing water."

The engine was started, lines were cast off, and Captain Gunn manoeuvred the boat away from the dock. They chugged slowly along the harbour until they reached the fuel dock, where they were able to top up their fuel and water before letting go again and heading out into Burrard Inlet.

The crew lined the rails, and with Captain Gunn at the wheel they headed out into the harbour, passing a small island on their left.

"That's Deadman's Island," he said. "The Natives used to use it to bury their dead. Put them in cedar boxes up trees. They've cut down all the trees now and put a sawmill there instead. Crying shame. Shouldn't have been allowed. Very disrespectful to the Natives. And over there is Stanley Park. Pity we didn't have more time in Vancouver; it's a lovely spot."

After passing the island they swung around Brockton Point and headed for the entrance into Burrard Inlet.

"They're going to start building a bridge across to West Vancouver next year," said Captain Gunn as he set his course towards the narrows. "They've been talking about it for years, but finally decided on a huge suspension bridge so that all the shipping can pass underneath. It's going to be a marvel. Look, you can see the engineers and surveyors working on the shore deciding where exactly the footings are going to go."

There was quite a current swirling in the narrows, but they had it going with them and passed through the gap with several other boats taking advantage of the tide. Soon they were out in English Bay with the city appearing from behind the trees of Stanley Park on their left, the rising mound of Point Grey in the distance, and the wooded shores of West Vancouver on their starboard side.

"Mostly cottages over there right now, but they say there'll be lots of development once the bridge is built," said Captain Gunn as he lit up his pipe. "Hard to imagine—it's pretty much total wilderness right now."

It was a glorious summer day, and West Vancouver's shores sloped sharply skywards until they became the jagged peaks of the North Shore mountains. Vancouver and its suburbs were truly perched on the edge of a great wilderness, and the children felt very small against all the vastness of sea, sky, and mountains.

Once they were well away from the narrows and out in the middle of English Bay, Captain Gunn set the crew to raising the sails. It took both Molly and Ian at the main halyard, and Sophie and Leticia at the foresail halyard, to get the sails raised fully and halyards tightened. Harriet and Mark were able to manage the jib and staysail, and finally the sheets were all adjusted and secured and *South Islander* headed out towards Georgia Strait on a beam reach. Captain Gunn ordered Mark to cut the engine, and as the throbbing died away the wonderful sounds of a ship under sail took over. The gentle slap of the water on the hull, the occasional flap of canvas, and the gentle thrumming in the rigging were all sounds that the crew loved. Even Mark, that most assiduous of engineers, popped his head up from below decks with a grin.

"That's a marvellous engine," he said. "Just let me know when you need it again, and I can have it started in a minute. Jolly nice to be sailing, though!"

OVER THE NEXT few hours, the crew spent some time figuring out how the boat sailed, what sails needed trimming, who was going to do what, and generally how they were going to work together. Captain Gunn passed the wheel over to Ian and instructed him on the course to set and follow that would bring them to Porlier Pass.

"Just keep the needle slightly west of ssw," he instructed. "Try not to fall too far off that course, or else we'll have to beat back to get to the pass. Most days in the summer the wind is blowing from the northwest, just like today, so that will give us a great reach across the Strait."

Sophie disappeared below and reappeared half an hour later with lunch.

"I thought we should have a really good feast for our first meal. Soup, pemmican sandwiches, and tomatoes. Tea and biscuits to finish up."

The crew joined Ian and Captain Gunn in the cockpit and passed around the sandwiches, drinking their soup out of large china mugs.

"I've been learning how to make bread," said Sophie. "I think I can do it in that stove. I'd like to try because we might not be able to get fresh bread all the time."

"Good idea," said Captain Gunn. "You can put it to rise on top of the engine where it will keep nice and warm. Now, I think Sophie as chief cook should be spared all washing up, so the rest of you can take turns cleaning up after meals. We'll make a rota for on-board duties."

After lunch Captain Gunn stretched himself along one side of the cockpit for his afternoon nap, and the others spread themselves over the cabin top and foredeck to enjoy the sail. It took almost six hours to cross Georgia Strait, but finally they were approaching Porlier Pass, the tidal gap between Galiano and Valdes Islands. Captain Gunn had spent an hour or so with the crew, instructing them on how to read the tide and current tables, and together they had calculated the exact time they needed to be at the pass.

"Think of Georgia Strait as a huge bathtub," he had said. "When the tide is flooding, it is gushing through all the gaps along these Gulf Islands, filling the tub. When the tide is ebbing, it's emptying out the bathtub into the inside waters we'll find on the other side of the pass. We need to get there just after slack, and use a little bit of the ebbing tide to help push us through."

And indeed they timed it perfectly. *South Islander*, with her engine ticking over in case the wind failed them, slid through the pass and found herself on the other side, with myriad small islands around them. They turned north and by tea time found themselves passing Ruxton Island and approaching Pirates Cove on De Courcy Island. Ian and Molly studied the chart and noted that the entrance was a little tricky with a rocky promontory jutting out at the turning point into the cove. As they were now on a falling tide they needed to be very careful, not only for the underwater rocks at the entrance, but also for the narrow channel into the cove, with very shallow water on either side.

"Look," said Harriet. "There are leading marks painted on the rocks, just like the boat harbour at Plockton." Everyone looked at the two painted arrows pointing towards each other.

"When they line up it's safe to turn, according to the chart," said Molly. "Then we can turn smartly to port and aim for the end of the cove. We need to stay parallel to this shore and about twenty feet off it."

The sails were lowered, Mark started the engine, and with the crew posted as lookouts on either side and at the bow, *South Islander* crept into the cove. Once inside, Captain Gunn circled a couple of times, scoping out a good place to drop the anchor. Finally, he called to Mark to put the boat into reverse. Ian let go the anchor chain, and as it rattled out of the chain locker the boat went slowly backwards until Captain Gunn called for the anchor rode to be secured. *South Islander* slid to a halt, and once Captain Gunn was sure the anchor was secure, Mark cut the engine.

Quiet descended on the boat as they surveyed their surroundings. They were the only boat in the most perfect of anchorages. The shores were edged with rocks, and the terrain was covered with a mixture of vegetation, including the strange reddish barked trees they had noticed earlier on other islands they had passed.

"I can hardly believe this is where Brother XII actually lived," said Harriet. "We should go ashore and find his farm. That's the place to start looking for the treasure."

"Not tonight," said Captain Gunn. "It's getting late, and we should have supper and bed down. Exploring and treasure hunting start first thing tomorrow!"

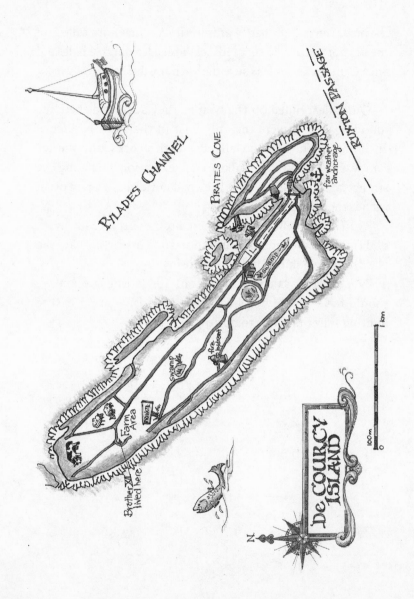

PYLADES CHANNEL

RUXTON PASSAGE

PIRATES COVE

fair weather anchorage

swamp

swamp

fire hydrant

PRIVATE

Farm Area

Brother XII lived here

De COURCY ISLAND

N

100m · 1 km

CHAPTER FOUR
THE STORY OF BROTHER XII

T HE CREW WERE awakened in the morning by the sound of rapping on the side of the hull. As they sleepily tumbled out of their bunks, they heard Captain Gunn talking to someone. After a few minutes he put his head down the companionway.

"Wakey, wakey, you sleepyheads! We've got company. Sophie, can you make a pot of coffee as well as some tea for the rest of us? Apparently people drink coffee first thing in the morning on this side of the Atlantic! Funny habit, if you ask me, but best humour the locals!"

Sophie chivvied the others to get washed and dressed and tidy the cabins while the kettle was boiling. Then she sent Leticia up ahead with milk, sugar, and biscuits on a tray and Ian with the enamel coffee pot. She followed with the tea.

"Hello," she said to the visitor. "I hope the coffee is all right. I haven't had much experience making it, but I followed the instructions on the packet."

The visitor was settled comfortably in the cockpit and it was all the children could do not to stare at him. However, they were all very well brought up and managed to hide their surprise at his appearance.

He was about thirty years old but looked older as he was sporting a massive beard and long, wild hair. He was barefoot and dressed in a tattered pair of trousers, roughly cut off at midcalf, and an old shirt with holes in the elbows. His dinghy, now floating astern at the end of its painter, was in terrible condition with peeling paint, an old shredded rope fender around the gunwale, and a mismatched pair of oars.

"This is Joe Absolom," said Captain Gunn. "I've been telling him that we are interested in Brother XII and his treasure, and he has a very interesting story to tell us."

"Did you know him?" said Harriet, hardly believing that she could actually be talking to someone who had met the man she'd read so much about.

"Yes, I did, and sorely wished I'd never set eyes on him. Proper wicked he was, and it's not only me and you that would like to catch up to him."

"Oh, do tell us what you know," piped up Leticia. "We've come such a long way, and we would really love to hear all about a real live villain."

"Let the poor man have his coffee first before you interrogate him," said Captain Gunn. "How would you like it?"

"Black, no sugar," answered their guest. When he was settled with his cup of coffee, he began his story.

"I worked in a hardware store in Victoria," he began, "happily married for three years, and we had a nice little house. I used to cycle to work every day, and my wife, Maggie, stayed home and kept things neat around the house. I didn't realize that she had started going to these meetings with Brother XII. He sold himself as some sort of guru, lots of praying and telling them—mostly young women like my wife—that he had the answer to all their problems. I only found out about this later, because the first thing I knew was that I got home one day and she was gone. And so were all our savings that I had stashed under the floorboards. Never did trust banks. Anyway, she was gone and I had no idea where. The police weren't much help; they just said she was a grown woman and could go where she pleased. I did a lot of asking around and found several other men whose wives had also disappeared. In the end we were able to track them down to here, to a big farm at the north end of this island. Me and several of the other husbands came tearing up here to get our wives back, but they refused to leave Brother XII. We even had a hard time trying to speak to them. We were met at the gate by an armed guard who wouldn't let us onto the property. Eventually, my wife and a few of the others whose husbands had come along with me agreed to come to the gate and talk to us. But it didn't do any good. They were well and truly hooked by the evil man, said that now their lives had 'purpose.'"

"That's terrible," breathed Harriet. "What did you do next? Call the police to get her back?"

"Wasn't no point. They'd already said that they were all grown women and could do what they wanted. And as far as the money goes, my wife could argue it was hers as much as mine, and she had a right to give it away."

"So is she still there—on the farm?" said Molly. "We could mount a raid and get her back!"

"Well, that's the next part of the story," said Joe. "The other husbands decided that they had to go back to their jobs, but I just couldn't leave without my Maggie. So I found an old cabin—you can see it over there in the trees—and just moved in. Didn't have any money, but the other husbands gave me a bit to live on while I kept an eye on the farm. There seemed to be more and more people arriving, even couples, and then things started to get out of hand. Brother XII had a most unpleasant consort, a woman they called Madame Z. Sometimes I hid in the bushes by the fence and listened to people talking. I heard about beatings from Madame Z and Brother XII's henchmen, and then they started to fortify the farm with great high fences and armed guards all around. Anyway, eventually the police came calling because some people had escaped and told tales of what had been going on. They wanted their money back too. One night there was a big commotion out in the cove, where Brother XII had his boat anchored. I paddled out in my dinghy but kept my distance because some of the men were toting guns. Out into Pylades Channel they went, and then there was a huge bang and the boat went up in flames. Burned to the waterline, it did, but I'm pretty sure Brother XII and his companions got away in one of the boats. In any case, no one has heard from him since, and all the money disappeared with him.

Of course, I ran like the devil up to the farm, and it was crawling with police and people milling around, weeping and wailing. Most of the buildings had been smashed and burned, and the place was a mess. I found my Maggie sitting on the ground staring into space. Wouldn't talk to me or anyone else. I brought her back to the cabin, but she just sat on a chair rocking back and forth. The other husbands were able to take their wives back to Victoria. Had a hard time readjusting, but most of them did all right. Not my Maggie, though. Eventually I had to take her to Nanaimo and put her in the mental hospital. She's there now. I didn't have the heart to go back to my job, so I just stayed here. I do a bit of fishing, mend nets for fishermen, odd jobs over on Vancouver Island from time to time, but really I've turned into a hermit. Brother XII ruined my life and Maggie's life and the lives of lots of others. I'd really like to track him down and have him thrown in jail, but to tell the truth, I'm pretty tired and it's easier just to stay here. I go and visit Maggie once a month, but she doesn't recognize me and she's never spoken a word from that day to this."

Captain Gunn and the others were silent as they absorbed this story. What were they to do? The children looked at Joe and tried to imagine what it would be like to have one of their family members walk away from their home like Joe's wife had done. Somehow the game of finding treasure had turned into a real-life tragedy.

Leticia spoke up. "Do you have any idea of what might have happened to him?"

"Did anyone try to find him or the gold?" asked Molly.

"What does it matter about the gold?" scolded Harriet, shooting Molly a look. "What matters is that Maggie has never recovered. Maybe there's something we could do to help Joe."

Finally Joe spoke again.

"Of course, because of the treasure, lots of people went out looking for Brother XII, but no one turned up any sign of him or the money. I did hear later that before he ended up on De Courcy Island, Brother XII had been involved in the rum-running trade during the Prohibition years. Made him lots of money even before he started stealing from his followers. I've heard that one of his rum-running buddies is living up the coast. Retired from the proceeds and built himself a nice place on one of the islands farther north. Mink Island, I think it's called. Perhaps you should go calling and have a chat with him."

"That's a wizard idea," said Molly jumping up. "But first I think we should all go and have a look at the farm. Maybe we'll find some clues there."

"Hold your horses, Molly," said Captain Gunn. "Joe, are you sure you want us to go looking?" Suddenly, leading a group of children on a treasure hunt while this poor man's wife was locked up in an asylum seemed to be in bad taste.

Joe looked pensive for a few minutes and sat with his now cold cup of coffee cradled in his hands.

"You know, I think it will make me feel better, not worse, if you go digging for him and his treasure. Not that the money means anything to me anymore, but maybe if I'm able to tell Maggie that we know what happened it will bring her around."

"So the hunt is still on!" burst out Molly, trying—and not exactly succeeding—to contain her glee in light of Joe's sad story. "Let's go and take a look at that farm. Joe, can you come with us?"

"Sure thing," said Joe. "I'll meet you on-shore in an hour."

THE WALK TO the farm took them along a beautiful forested trail, which wound through the dense salal bushes that covered the forest floor.

"There's a few cabins along the west side of the island, facing Vancouver Island," said Joe as they walked briskly along. "Some folks like to come on weekends, but the place has a sinister history, and not too many people come ashore here. There are lots of other islands to choose from if you fancy a summer cabin."

Occasionally they glimpsed the ocean through the trees, and after about half an hour they arrived at a fence resembling a stockade from the days of the Wild West. The road ended at an enormous gate made of driftwood. Everything, however, was in total disrepair. The fence was knocked down in several places and the gate was hanging off its hinges.

They all stepped through the gateway and paused to survey their surroundings. At first glance it was an idyllic spot, with large areas of pasture and sheep grazing peacefully. However, as they walked along the road, they noticed that not one of the many buildings was intact. Some were just a pile of lumber, others were charred, with gaping holes where there had once been doors and windows, and the largest of the buildings had no roof.

"That one there was the dining room and lecture hall," said Joe pointing at the large building. "It's only been three years since he left, but Brother XII and his cohorts smashed a lot before they went, and the rest has been pulled apart by folks wanting free building supplies. In its heyday it was a pretty busy place. Brother XII and Madame Z worked those poor folks like slaves. They had cows and sheep and worked the land. They grew a huge vegetable garden, and they used to send the most trusted members in a rowboat over to Boat Harbour on Vancouver Island with produce to sell. Poor Maggie had to work in the dairy. She was up at the crack of dawn to milk, then she had to make butter and cheese, muck out the barn—she used to work eighteen hours a day."

They wandered around the derelict buildings, not quite knowing where to start looking for clues to the treasure.

"I'll show you the most interesting bit," said Joe as he led them around the back of the dining hall to a small shed that still had two walls standing, one with a barred window. "This is where he kept the gold. He had guards posted day and night, of course. Rumour has it that he turned all that he was given by members into gold coins and packed them into Mason jars. Dug a huge room under that hut, reinforced it with steel bars, and had a great iron lid on the whole thing. When the police got here, Brother XII and Madame Z had already left, and the lid to the cellar was open. Come and have a look."

No one needed a second invitation. They all gathered in the broken hut. With the aid of a flashlight (thoughtfully brought along by Mark), they looked down through the opening in the floor. What was revealed was a large hole in the ground. Just that. No shelves, no proper walls or floor, and certainly no gold. The most interesting thing about the hole, however, was what was written on the underside of the lid, now propped open against one of the remaining walls. Written in chalk in large capital letters was this message:

LOOK ALL YOU LIKE! YOU WON'T FIND THE GOLD OR ME UNTIL WE MEET IN THE GREAT HEREAFTER. IF YOU'RE LOOKING FOR A CLUE YOU'RE OUT OF LUCK! BAD LUCK TO ALL YOU TREASURE HUNTERS!

"Well, that's not going to put us off," said Molly stubbornly. "I think Joe's right. Brother XII jumped ship after starting that fire, and now he's hiding out somewhere up the coast, counting his ill-gotten gains and generally being a horrible person to anyone unlucky enough to encounter him. Come on, we're just wasting time here. Let's get going and find that rum-runner fellow!"

A COUPLE OF HOURS later, after getting everything aboard ship-shape and sharing lunch with Joe, Ian raised the anchor using the capstan on the foredeck, Mark put the engine in gear, and they slipped out of the cove.

"We'll let you know what happens!" yelled Molly from the foredeck as Joe sat in his dinghy in the middle of the cove. "We'll find him, don't worry, and we'll bring you back your share of the gold."

"We're in perfect time for getting through Dodd Narrows," said Leticia, who had been studying the tide and current tables. "It's fun figuring this stuff out."

Not that he mistrusted his niece, but knowing that her grasp of mathematics was rather tenuous, Captain Gunn checked her calculations.

"Jolly good, Leticia," he chuckled. "We'll make a mariner of you yet!"

Leticia went pink with pleasure at having figured out slack tide without the help of Ian or her uncle, and her calculations were proved correct as they slipped through the narrows between Mudge Island to their starboard and Vancouver Island on their port side. They came out on the other side into Northumberland Channel, and the wind, which had been almost non-existent since they had left the island, picked up and turned into a very brisk breeze blowing right down the channel onto their nose.

"I think we'll keep the engine going rather than beating into this. We don't want to spend all day getting to Nanaimo. I've heard there's a wonderful place to anchor just across from the harbour. Newcastle Island, it's called, and we can anchor there overnight even in the strongest of winds."

The weather had started to close in as they neared their intended anchorage in Mark Bay, just off Newcastle Island. By the time the anchor was set and the deck tidied up it had started to rain in earnest. Captain Gunn lit the little wood stove, and the whole crew sat around the saloon table talking about poor

Joe and his tales of Brother XII's nefarious deeds. It was warm and cozy in the cabin as everyone sipped on mugs of hot cocoa.

"I still think it's a bit callous to be looking for treasure when poor Joe is sitting in that little cabin waiting for Maggie to recover her wits," said Sophie.

"Didn't you hear what Joe said?" exclaimed Molly, jumping up in her eagerness to get her point across. "He said it might make Maggie better if he could tell her we'd at least found their stolen life savings."

"Let's put it to the vote," said Ian. "All those in favour of going after the treasure, raise your hands."

There was silence for a few minutes as everyone aboard pondered the pros and cons of hunting for the gold. Molly was the first to raise her hand, followed by Mark, Leticia, and Ian. Posy didn't really understand why they were voting, so she didn't put up her hand until she could see which side was going to win. Harriet and Sophie hesitated longer than anyone else, but at last they too slowly raised their hands. Captain Gunn didn't participate in the vote. He trusted his crew to make the right decision.

"I think it really might help to lay some ghosts to rest if we can at least find out what happened to Brother XII, even if we don't find any trace of the money," said Harriet.

"Well, I'm not giving up on finding the treasure," said Molly. "Did you see that shack that Joe was living in? Finding even some of the money would help him get back on his feet."

"All right," said Captain Gunn. "It seems we are all in agreement. Now it's time to plan the next few days."

He spread out the charts on the table. "The first thing is to see if we can track down the rum-runner and find out what he knows. I've heard it's pretty gorgeous scenery up near that Mink Island, so even if we don't find him or any hint of Brother XII and his treasure, it will be a beautiful cruise."

"That sounds rather defeatist," said Molly. "Of course we'll find the rum-runner, and of course he'll want to tell us all he knows. A beautiful cruise is for old fogies—we're explorers and pirates!"

Captain Gunn eyed his niece. How much of her character and interests he could take credit for, he wasn't sure, but on the whole he was glad that between him and his sister, Fiona, they had raised such a tough character. Nothing much was going to get in the way of Molly getting what she wanted out of life. And right now what she wanted was to find pirate gold. He would do what he could to help her and the others at least have a good try at recovering the treasure.

"Depending on the weather, we'll head across Georgia Strait to Pender Harbour. If the wind isn't too strong it should be a pleasant sail. Pender Harbour is a good protected anchorage, and we can fill up on fuel and groceries before we head farther north. Here, take a look at the chart." He summoned everyone around the table. "It's quite a long slog from Pender Harbour up Malaspina Strait to Savary Island, and Lund on the BC mainland, but once we get there we'll be close to Desolation Sound and Mink Island."

"Why is it called Desolation Sound?" asked Sophie. "It doesn't sound a very nice place for a summer holiday."

"I know the answer to that," jumped in Harriet. "Apparently Captain Vancouver visited this area in 1792, and it must have been a rainy summer because he said... Hang on, I've got it written down in my notebook." Everyone waited as she rifled through her notes. Sophie caught Molly rolling her eyes and gave her a poke.

"Here it is!" exclaimed Harriet. "Vancouver said, 'There was not a single prospect that was pleasing to the eye.' I read all about it on the ship coming over."

"The human encyclopaedia strikes again," Ian said with a grin. The others sniggered, and Harriet turned beet red. Sometimes she got so caught up in her quest for knowledge that she didn't stop to consider that maybe not everyone would find something—like the observations of a long-dead explorer—as fascinating as she did.

"I think it's great that Harriet knows so much about the place," said Sophie, rushing to Harriet's defence like a mother hen. "It wouldn't be the same if we just sailed through without any idea of who was here first."

"I think you'll find that Captain Vancouver wasn't the first one here by a long shot," said Captain Gunn. "The Native people have lived here for thousands of years, and they have had a pretty rough time of it ever since the explorers first arrived."

"Well, on a day like today I think I might agree with Captain Vancouver," said Leticia as she peered out of one of the portholes at the grey skies and drizzle.

The crew had had enough of history lessons. They pulled out the packs of cards to play a rowdy game of Racing Demons.

FORTUNATELY FOR THE expedition, bad weather in the summer time on the BC coast was usually short-lived. After an early night and long sleep, the crew awoke the next morning to bright blue skies and a brisk breeze.

They took their breakfast (a hearty bowl of porridge studded with raisins and served with plenty of sugar and cream) on deck and watched the activity on-shore. They could see a large red pavilion near the top of the dock, where a steamship was tied up. It appeared that the ship was being used as a hotel, and they could see passengers strolling along the decks and passing up and down the gangplank on their way to the pavilion and the facilities on-shore. Even at this early hour, they could see people playing croquet on the large field and others setting off for walks along the island's wooded trails. It looked like a very tame place for a holiday, given that they themselves were on the hunt for pirate treasure, but, as Molly said, there was no accounting for tastes.

Soon they had weighed anchor and were heading up Newcastle Channel between the island and Nanaimo, passing docks and shipyards on the city side of the channel and weaving between boat traffic coming and going along the narrow waterway. Before long, they had swung around the northern end of Newcastle Island and were heading out into Georgia Strait.

"We need to be very careful out here," said Ian, studying the chart. "There are loads of rocks and little islands, but once we've navigated through those we can set a course for the southern end of Texada Island."

Soon, with all sails set and the engine cut, they were sailing briskly across the strait. Captain Gunn was pleased to see that the crew was shaking down well and everyone knew their jobs. Molly and Ian were good sailors, and after a few days at sea the captain was confident they could safely sail the boat themselves if necessary.

"It does rather seem like we are back-tracking," said Leticia. "This is the second time we've crossed Georgia Strait, but of course we had to go and see De Courcy Island for ourselves."

After several hours of very good sailing, and another delicious lunch served on deck by Sophie, with Leticia and Posy helping pass things through the hatch, *South Islander* passed the southernmost tip of Texada Island and changed course to the north towards Pender Harbour. They sailed close-hauled for a while against the increasingly strong wind coming down Malaspina Strait from the northwest, and finally Captain Gunn gave Mark permission to fire up the engine. Sails were stowed and they set a direct course that took them between two small islands and into Pender Harbour. Immediately, the wind dropped to nothing, and they chugged quietly along until dropping the anchor in Hospital Bay.

Sophie wanted to buy some yeast for her bread-baking experiment, and there were a few other things on the grocery list, so Sophie, Leticia, Harriet, Posy, and Mark rowed over to the little settlement of Irvine's Landing in the dinghy, while Ian, Molly, and Captain Gunn stayed on-board and looked over the charts. As well as the items on her list, Sophie came back with a large package of fresh lamb chops, and with the potatoes and fresh vegetables they already had on-board, she and her assistant (that evening it was Leticia) cooked a feast fit for royalty. Despite the sunshine, it had been a cool and breezy day after the rain of the day before, but they still decided to eat outside. Mark and Ian put up the cockpit table, and soon everyone was enjoying the slap-up meal. Captain Gunn opened a bottle of beer, and the rest of the crew drank lemonade.

"Only a small tide runs down Malaspina Strait, but we might as well have it with us rather than against us, so we'll weigh anchor at 6:00 a.m. and have breakfast on the go," said Captain Gunn as he settled back on the cushions with his post-dinner pipe and glass of whisky. "Bit of a slog up the coast here with not much of interest to stop for, but I think we'll tie up at Lund tomorrow night and then we'll be in good shape to make Mink Island the next day."

The clean-up crew served Sophie and Leticia tea. As chief cook and assistant cook, the two girls were allowed to sip their hot drinks lounging in comfort with Captain Gunn, while the rest of the crew washed dishes and tidied up down below, accompanied by Molly singing a selection of fine pirate songs. Her favourite went like this:

> Fifteen men on the dead man's chest—
> Yo-ho-ho, and a bottle of rum!
> Drink and the devil had done for the rest—
> Yo-ho-ho, and a bottle of rum!

The mate was fixed by the bosun's pike
The bosun' brained with a marlin spike
And Cookey's throat was marked belike
It had been gripped by fingers ten;
And there they lay all good dead men
Like break o' day in a boozing ken—
Yo-ho-ho, and a bottle of rum!

Molly soon had the whole crew laughing and joining in the refrain.

"I'm glad we're not the sort of pirates in the song," said Leticia. "I'd like to think we're more the Robin Hood kind of pirates putting things right."

"It's just a song," said Molly, "and a jolly fine one at that! Makes the washing up go quicker."

With an early start in the morning, and a long day on the water behind them, the crew settled down to an early night without too much complaint. Except for Mark, who wanted to check over the engine one more time.

"You never know when we might need to start it in a hurry," he said, reaching for his bag of oily rags.

"You're going to kill that engine with love," chuckled Captain Gunn. "Leave it now, and you'll be the first to know when we need it tomorrow."

After taking a last look at the night sky studded with stars and with a sickle moon hanging over the entrance to the harbour, everyone settled in for the night. It wasn't long before the sound of Captain Gunn's snores lulled everyone to sleep.

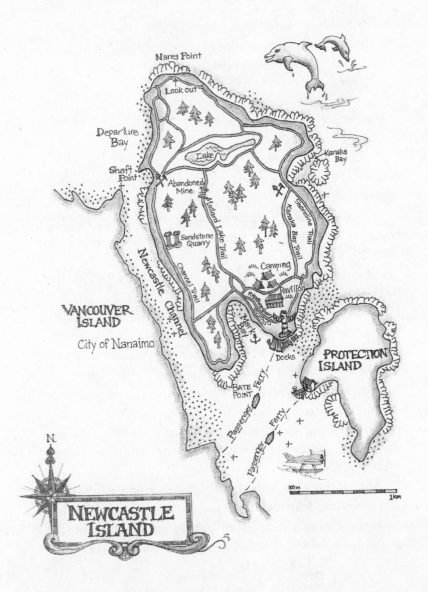

Nares Point

Look out

Departure
Bay

Kanaka
Bay

Shaft
Point

Abandoned
Mine

Lake

Mallard Lake Trail

Shoreline Trail

Kanaka Bay Trail

Sandstone
Quarry

Channel Trail

Camping

Pavilion

Newcastle Channel

Mark
Bay

VANCOUVER
ISLAND

City of Nanaimo

Docks

PROTECTION
ISLAND

Bate
Point

Passenger Ferry

Passenger Ferry

N.

100m

1km

**NEWCASTLE
ISLAND**

CHAPTER FIVE

HOT ON THE TRAIL

BY 8:00 the next morning, *South Islander*, with all sails set, was on a broad reach heading north up Malaspina Strait. The bulk of Texada Island rose on their port side and the mainland, dotted with cottages, stretched north and south on their starboard side. It was a wonderful day for a sail, with a brisk and constant breeze from the southeast.

"That's good news for us," said Captain Gunn. "I've heard that this stretch can be a real slog with the wind often right on the nose at this time of year. Funnels down this strait, it does, and pretty miserable, even in mid-summer. We'll hope the wind is blowing the other way when it's time to head south again."

After breakfast Mark got his first turn out at the end of the bowsprit, securely tethered in case he fell. Suddenly he yelled and pointed at something in the distance, almost slipping off in the process.

"Look, look! What are they?"

Everyone rushed to the rail and peered where Mark was pointing. Three black-and-white creatures, each about the size of a large pig, were cruising along with the boat. They rode the

bow wave and dove under the boat, and one of them jumped clean out of the water as the crew watched in awe.

"Run below and grab the book on British Columbia wildlife," said Captain Gunn.

Harriet flew down the companionway and reached for the book, which was sandwiched on the shelf along with the tide tables and other reference books that had come with the boat. She flicked through the pages and quickly found a picture of the creatures.

"They're Dall's porpoises," she said, "related to whales, but much smaller, of course. The book says they are quite common round here."

They watched the porpoises follow along with the boat for another half hour or so, until the creatures spied something more interesting and took off at breakneck speed.

"I'm going to keep a list of all the wildlife we see," said Harriet. "The book says there's a chance of seeing orca whales. They are more common farther north, but we might be lucky. And seals and sea lions are common. It's hard to believe we're seeing these in the wild, rather than in the zoo."

A couple of hours later the boat and its crew were approaching the entrance to the harbour at Lund. They had passed the sandy sliver of Savary Island, which was directly across the channel from Lund, and decided that they would try to go ashore and explore it on their way back. Finding Brother XII and his treasure was foremost in all their minds, and nobody felt like taking a break now to lie on the beaches of Savary. The island had been touted in one of the boat's guidebooks as having some of the best sandy beaches anywhere in North America, but he was the only one of the crew who was fond of baking in the sun.

The harbour master in Lund helped them find a good spot on the dock and assured them that the hotel served a very good meal.

"We'll treat ourselves to a slap-up dinner," said Captain Gunn. "I hope they have a good selection of beer."

They were soon all seated around a big table in the dining room of the hotel, which was a gathering spot for loggers and settlers. The restaurant was full. There were some rather rough-looking characters sitting at the bar, cracking jokes and laughing loudly enough to wake the dead. Sitting alone at a table by the window was a man surrounded by reference books. He was writing furiously in a notebook, barely noticing the noise around him. Harriet was intrigued.

"What's he writing about?" she wondered out loud, craning her neck to get a closer look.

"That's Jim Spilsbury," said the waiter, appearing at the table to take their orders. "He's a whiz at making and mending radio telephones."

Mark's ears perked up at the mention of a fellow lover of mechanical instruments. He leaned backwards in his chair to try to catch a glimpse of the diagrams and equations in Mr. Spilsbury's notebook. Sophie grabbed the arm of his chair just as it was about to topple over and send Mark flying.

"He sells them to fishing and logging camps," the waiter continued, "and some of the bigger forestry boats have them on-board. Real handy they are. Means that folks out in the wilderness can stay in touch. Lives over there on Savary Island. He's a real eccentric—flies up into those remote inlets in an old float plane. Surprised he hasn't killed himself!"

"Golly," said Molly, "that would be an adventure all right. Taking off and landing on the water. You could go anywhere!"

"Well, for now you'll have to make do with floating, not flying," said Captain Gunn, "and I think we should all hit our bunks right after dinner. All this fresh air is making me pretty tired, and we need to have our wits about us if we want to make friends with the rum-runner Joe told us about. He's the key to finding our villain."

After a delicious dinner of roast beef and baked potatoes, followed by apple pie and ice cream, the crew had to admit they were feeling tired. The boat was beginning to seem like home, and they were soon tucked up in their berths. It didn't take long for everyone to be sound asleep, dreaming of villainous tricksters and chests full of gold.

THEY AWOKE THE next morning to the smell of fresh-baked bread. Sophie had mixed up a batch the evening before and crept out of her bunk while the rest of the crew was still sound asleep to knead it and put it in the oven, which she managed to light without any help—quite a tricky job.

Her early start was rewarded by the enthusiastic response she got to her loaf, which they had for breakfast spread with lashings of butter and a thick layer of marmalade. Breakfast was washed down, as usual, with gallons of tea. Soon after, they cast off their mooring lines and headed out, turning quickly to starboard and aiming for Sarah Point at the end of the Malaspina Peninsula.

They passed a tug and log boom heading south in Thulin Passage and from there reached Sarah Point, rounding it and setting a course for Mink Island. Once they rounded the point, the incredible vista of snow-capped mountains rearing up from the forested slopes below, the sparkling water dotted with islands large and small, and the fact that they seemed to be the only boat for miles around left the crew speechless. Despite their previous adventures, including a good smattering of foreign travel, it was quite unlike anything they had ever seen before. It is true that Scotland has plenty of sea lochs dotted with islands, as well as grand and imposing mountains, but now that wild and impressive scenery seemed very tame.

"I think they should rename this place," said Harriet, glancing up from the chart she was studying. "It doesn't deserve to be called Desolation Sound. Maybe Spectacular Sound?"

The chart was spread out on the deck, and everyone had a good look. It was clear that it would take months, not the weeks they had, to explore every nook and cranny looking for signs of Brother XII. The area was dotted with islands, anchorages large and small, and the mainland itself, which stretched more than four thousand miles to the east. They all felt rather overwhelmed by the enormity of the task they had set themselves.

"It's obvious we're not going to find him without some help, so let's go and find our rum-runner and hope he's talkative," said Captain Gunn. "Look, you can see Mink Island not too far ahead."

South Islander sailed over a sea so clear and blue that, except for the absence of palm trees, it could have been in the Caribbean. Soon they approached a thickly wooded island. They rounded a point, dropped the sails, and quietly slipped into a neat little bay. Through the trees they could see a roof, and there was a small dock with a motorboat and a rowing boat tied up to it.

The anchor was dropped, all lines and sheets neatly coiled, and the dinghy brought alongside. Two trips from ship to shore found the entire crew walking up the dock towards the roof of the building. Along the way they noticed several "no trespassing" signs, and as they continued along the forested path they saw that it was not just one roof but several. The collection of a main house and outbuildings was surrounded by a sturdy stockade fence. The gate in the fence stood open—perhaps a sign that they would get a friendly reception—and they continued up the path to the front door of the main building.

The house looked like a cross between a wizard's castle and a pirate's lair, with a maritime museum thrown in for good measure. Full of odd angles, stairs that seemed to go nowhere, portholes for windows, and balconies and decks crowded with various bits and pieces, it seemed to have been put together and added onto with no plan in mind. The whole effect was quite charming.

They mounted the steps to the front door thinking that whoever lived there must be a very interesting character indeed.

"Do you think he'll look like a pirate?" asked Posy, sounding both thrilled at the prospect and a little bit worried.

"I hope so. I've never met a real-life pirate!" said Molly. "Except for myself, of course."

"It doesn't look like a pirate's house," said Harriet, "more like the house of someone really eccentric."

"He might just want to live a solitary life without visitors," said Sophie, always the voice of reason. "We did ignore his 'no trespassing' signs."

The doorbell had obviously come off a ship, as it was engraved with the name ss *Indigo*. Mark stepped up and pulled the braided cord.

For a couple of minutes there was silence from inside the house, and Mark was just about to give the bell another go when they heard a voice coming from the depths of the building.

"Whatever you're selling, I don't need it. And whatever you want, I don't have it. So just go away!"

The crew looked at each other. They had come a long way, and if the rum-runner wouldn't see them, they were right out of ideas. The thought of going home without having discovered anything new about Brother XII and his treasure was too disappointing for words.

"I'll have a go," said Molly. "A rum-runner's a kind of pirate, so perhaps it will just take one pirate talking to another pirate."

Captain Gunn nodded in agreement, and Molly stepped up to the door.

"Ahoy there, I'm Molly MacTavish, brave pirate and terror of the seas. I've come across the great ocean to see you, and I hope you will let me come in and talk to you."

Another silence followed, and then came the sound of footsteps. The door opened and the rum-runner was revealed—and he wasn't a bit like they had thought he would be! Far from being the piratical figure they had imagined, this fellow would have looked right at home in a suburban garden, sitting in a deckchair reading the newspaper, or maybe even mowing the lawn. He was neatly dressed in corduroy trousers, a flannel shirt, and a tie. His feet were clad in polished brogues, and he sported a trimmed beard and round spectacles. He looked like a bank clerk at home on the weekend.

"Not sure who you think you are, or what you think you want from me, but whatever it is, I can't help. I'm assuming at least one of you can read. Didn't you see the 'no trespassing' signs?"

There was a moment of silence and then everyone started speaking at once.

"We heard you knew Brother xii," said Molly.

"We've come ever such a long way—all the way from England," said Posy.

"We're really sorry to disturb you, but we've run out of other people to ask," said Sophie.

"We're pirates too," that was Molly again, "and we thought you were the best person to ask. Being a pirate yourself, of course."

At that, the rum-runner seemed to relax. Taking a look at the eager faces of the children and the apologetic face of Captain Gunn, he relented.

"All right," he said. "I'll give you half an hour of my time. I'm retired, you know, and I like to spend my days reading and gardening. Don't get many visitors, nor do I want any, but you look like an interesting bunch, so come in. My name's Jasper Peabody, by the way."

Everyone introduced themselves and followed Jasper into his house. The inside was as interesting as the outside, with stacks of books, old marine instruments, even the wheelhouse of an old boat that served as a cupboard for hats, coats, and boots. He led them into a large room furnished with an assortment of furniture, from elaborately carved oriental chests to more traditional English antiques, with a few bits and pieces built out of driftwood.

"Have a seat, and then let's hear what you're all up to and why you want to know about Brother XII."

Harriet recounted the story as they knew it so far, with reference to poor Joe on De Courcy Island.

"We would so love to find the treasure and return it to Joe and the others that Brother XII stole from," finished Harriet.

"What's in it for you lot?" asked Jasper.

"We're in it for the adventure," answered Molly. "Tracking down a dastardly villain and returning his ill-gotten gains to his victims seems a tremendous adventure to us."

"And I'll bet there's a reward," piped up Mark, before the others shushed him.

"I think there's a book to be written about this," added Captain Gunn. "As soon as I've finished my work on the Mounties, I'm going to get going on writing about Brother XII. It's a story with everything—gold, pirates, beautiful women, last-minute escapes, and much more that we hope you can tell us about."

Everyone could see that Jasper was thinking hard. They all kept silent whilst watching his face eagerly. Finally he spoke.

"I've been retired for quite a while," he began, "since 1933 actually, when Prohibition ended in the US. You may have heard about Prohibition, when all alcohol was banned in the US."

Coming from Britain, where even the smallest village boasted at least one pub, full every evening with locals socializing and consuming vast quantities of beer, the crew could barely imagine a country as large as the US banning the sale of alcohol.

"Anyway, Prohibition opened up a lot of opportunities for us in Canada, especially here in British Columbia, where it is easy to cross over to the US by water without anyone noticing. There were lots of small-time distilleries making whisky—and it wasn't just whisky. Those Americans were thirsty for champagne and fine French wines too. It was legal here, but the problem was how to get it across the border. Luckily for us, the coast over in Washington State has hundreds of beaches and coves perfect for landing the stuff. I started small, and when I began making a truckload of money, I invested in a purpose-built boat that could outrun most of the US Coast Guard boats. Tricky business it was, very competitive, with the bigger boats trying to put the smaller ones like mine out of business. Tip off the customs men, they would, in order to get their stuff to the US market with less competition. Anyway, I managed to do very well. My boat was very fast, but not so big that it was seen as much of a threat by the big boys. I'd pick up the booze down in Victoria and run across Juan de Fuca Strait into Washington State in the dead of night. Sometimes, I'd heave to a few miles offshore and we'd unload into small boats that had come out from the US shore. I had a good crew and most of them made some pretty serious money. Anyway, on one trip I was short a couple of crew and this man, said his name was Edward Wilson, approached me down at the dock and I took him on. Just one trip he did with us—he was a very weird character, and my other crewmembers didn't like him. At the end I paid him off, and that was the last we saw of him. But a couple of years later I started hearing rumours about him living on De Courcy Island with a bunch of 'followers.' Prohibition ended in 1933, and I decided to retire with my fortune and settle up here on Mink Island. I was travelling on my boat from Victoria, heading north, and I passed De Courcy Island. Thought I'd stop and see if the rumours were true. I anchored off the island and found my way to the farm. Asked to see Edward Wilson, and one of his cohorts at the gate said I'd better show some respect to Brother XII, as he was now known. 'All right,' I said, 'I'll show respect, but can I see him?' I was very curious by now; it all seemed pretty strange. The guard took me in to see Wilson, and he was sitting around surrounded by several young women, not doing much that I could see. So, we chatted for a while about this and that, and then I asked him about his setup. He got very cagey and started to get hostile, demanding to know why I was asking him all these questions. His guard started to get jumpy then, and I thought I'd better take my leave. As I was leaving, I was approached by a very handsome woman who invited me into her house to have a drink. I was tempted, I can tell you, but I decided that I'd best get out. She signalled the guard, and that's when I decided to make a run for it. Just made it to the gate when I heard a shot whizzing over my head. I hightailed it back to my boat and sailed away."

Jasper paused, as if just remembering something.

"There was one odd thing that Wilson asked me about during our conversation. He wanted to know if there were any places up the coast that might be for sale. I think he was thinking that if things got too hot for him, he'd like a bolthole. I told him about my island here and how remote it was, and I could see he was interested. In any case, that's the last I saw of him, but I certainly heard about all the fuss three years ago, only a few months after my visit to him, when he disappeared. I don't believe for a moment that he went down with that ship. Holed up somewhere, he is, enjoying all that ill-gotten gold."

The crew were silent, digesting this story. It seemed they might be on the right track, but Desolation Sound with all its islands, coves, and channels was a huge area to search. Where should they begin?

Jasper spoke again. "I reckon you might start asking questions in Refuge Cove. It's not far way, just across the sound on West Redonda Island. If he's around here somewhere, chances are someone will have heard rumours. He can't live without occasionally needing supplies from the outside world, and Refuge Cove has a store and post office. Hub of our little community it is. I go there myself every week or so."

Captain Gunn, who had been sitting quietly, riveted by Jasper's story, spoke up.

"You're a very interesting chap," he said somewhat unnecessarily. "Make a very good book, your story would. Are you interested in being the subject of a book?"

Jasper turned pink, took off his spectacles, polished them, and finally looked Captain Gunn in the eye.

"Never thought of myself as particularly interesting," he said, "but it would be nice to know that my story doesn't die with me. Never married or had kids, but I do have some nieces and nephews that will get my fortune when I go. I'd like them to know the stories of where it came from. I'm a bit of a hermit and they don't visit, but everyone likes to think they might not be forgotten the moment they die."

"Right," said Captain Gunn decidedly. "When we've found Brother xii and I've got rid of my crew"—he got a stern look from Molly at that comment—"I'll come back and we can chat again. I've almost finished my book on the Mounties, and my publisher is asking what's coming next. With ideas for two more books, I'll be able to enjoy tobacco and foreign travel for a while."

The crew invited Jasper back to *South Islander* for dinner, and after a delicious meal and an evening of more speculation on the whereabouts of Brother xii, the crew parted from their new friend and settled down for the night. Captain Gunn, however, was very late to bed. They could smell his pipe tobacco and hear him moving about the cockpit until well past midnight. Harriet woke up and looked at her watch with her flashlight.

Captain Gunn heard her moving about and peered down the companionway.

"Go to sleep, Harriet," he said. "I think we are well on the trail and we have our next stop figured out. We're sure to find some clues in Refuge Cove. I'm going to sleep now. We'll have another early start in the morning."

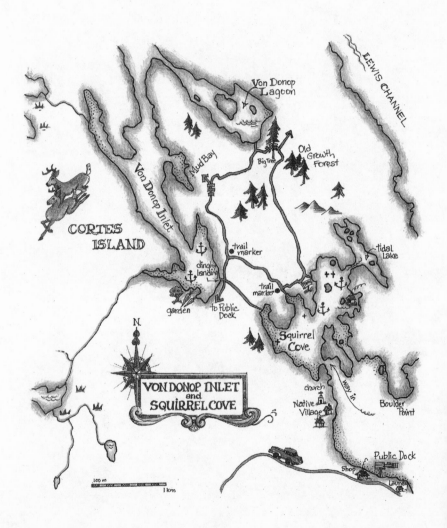

LEWIS CHANNEL

Von Donop
Lagoon

Mud Bay

Von Donop Inlet

Big Tree

Old Growth
Forest

tidal
Lake

CORTES
ISLAND

trail
marker

dinghy
landing

trail
marker

garden

to Public
Dock

Squirrel
Cove

N

VON DONOP INLET
and
SQUIRREL COVE

church

way in

Native
Village

Boulder
Point

100 m

1 km

Public Dock

Shop

Laundry

CHAPTER SIX

"WE'RE BEING FOLLOWED!"

B Y 10:00 A.M. the next day, *South Islander* was turning in to Refuge Cove. The cove bit deep into the mountainous terrain of West Redonda Island and was further protected by the island that lay in the middle of the cove. As *South Islander* came alongside the dock, Leticia and Molly jumped smartly ashore with the mooring lines and secured the boat with bow, stern, and spring lines.

A ramp led from the dock up to the general store, post office, and miscellaneous other buildings, all joined by a network of boardwalks. This was a place that appeared to be tethered to the rocky shore behind it, only needing someone to take out a support here or there for the whole thing to tumble into the cove. The crew walked up the ramp and along the boardwalk into the general store. It really was a *general* store, with a smattering of everything a boater could want. Tins and packets of food and barrels of potatoes and onions jostled for shelf space with fishing gear, books, and miscellaneous boat parts. There was a wooden counter, on top of which sat a large tabby cat, and a sign advertised stamps and mail delivery and drop-off. Behind the counter sat a little old woman with steel-rimmed glasses, a huge bun of hair on top of her head, and a colourful apron, its pockets bulging with scissors, string, labels, and other odds and ends. She sat in a comfortable armchair, knitting a scarf that seemed to have already reached an extraordinary length—almost long enough to reach down the dock to the boat, thought Posy, wondering who it was for and if she would have the courage to ask.

"Saw your boat come in," said the woman, putting down her knitting. "You want to watch out. There's some nasty-looking characters asking about you."

She pointed outside towards the dock, and on the very outside float, where it was hidden from *South Islander* by boats in between, they saw what she was pointing at. A very rundown motorboat with five men lounging on deck. Despite their proximity to the water, they all looked like they needed a bath. From the crew's viewpoint at the top of the ramp, they could see that four of the men were dark-haired with scruffy beards, while the fifth man was clean-shaven with a head of curly blond hair. He looked a lot younger than the others and seemed a bit out of place. All the men were dressed in an assortment of filthy, tattered, rags. Leticia wondering fleetingly if they had in fact snipped away at their own shirts and pants with garden shears to give them that perfect derelict look, intended to intimidate potential victims.

"Said they'd been talking to a fellow called Joe down on De Courcy Island who told them that a schooner with a crew of kids was heading this way to ask questions about Brother XII. You don't want to be getting yourselves mixed up with the likes of them. Very bad reputation, they have. Been caught a time or two pilfering off boats left at anchor."

"Mr. Peabody over on Mink Island said you might know something about Brother XII," said Leticia. "Do you have any idea where we might find him?"

"You don't want to go looking," cautioned the postmistress and storekeeper. "From all accounts he's a very bad character. He came in here a time or two, but that was a couple of years back. Haven't seen him for a while. Tell you what, though. There's a fellow over on Cortes Island who mentioned that he'd met him. Scared him half to death, he did, with his crew of toughs and that strange woman he always had with him."

"Whereabouts on Cortes could we find him?" asked Harriet.

"He has a small homestead in Von Donop Inlet," replied their new friend. "But watch out that those fellows down on the dock don't follow you there. I didn't tell them anything, but they saw you coming in and may decide to follow you if they get the chance."

THE CREW SAT around the cockpit eating another one of Sophie's excellent lunches, feeling a little let down by their lack of progress. Sophie sat quietly in a corner of the cockpit, looking glum for another reason altogether.

Captain Gunn was the only one who noticed. He got up from the table and approached her cautiously. Seeing her sitting there like that, he got a flashback of his sister, Fiona, when she was about Sophie's age, sulking in the corner and refusing to speak to anyone. The one and only time he'd attempted to cheer her up when she was in one of these moods, she returned the favour by boxing his ears. But this was different. Sophie seemed genuinely upset about something, and this time he was the adult in the situation. Not to mention the captain. He cleared his throat.

"Er... What's the matter, Sophie?"

The girl continued to stare intently at one spot on the mast, as if funnelling all her energy into one tiny, invisible space would keep her from falling apart. Alarmed, Captain Gunn saw that she was close to tears. There was nothing in the captain's manual about how to deal with this!

"It's not that I'm ungrateful," Sophie said finally. Her voice was shaky and she had to take a deep breath before continuing. "You've given me this fantastic opportunity to come all the way to Canada and have this great holiday..."

"But..." prompted Captain Gunn. He had absolutely no idea where she was going with this. Was she homesick? Seasick? Lovesick? Terrified of pirates? What on earth could it be?

"Well," she continued, finally mustering up the courage to turn away from her spot on the mast and look Captain Gunn in the eye. When she saw his bewildered expression, it triggered something inside her. All her good manners and etiquette lessons flew out the window (or rather the porthole), and everything that had been building up inside her since they set sail in Vancouver came flooding out.

"Frankly, Captain Gunn, it's not fair that all the others get to be explorers and adventurers while I slave away in the galley! They get to read maps and make all these exciting plans, and I have to pore over cookbooks and plan meals! I mean, honestly, Captain, did it ever occur to you—did you ever stop to think for one moment—that I might want to be an explorer, too, not just a cook?"

She stopped, realizing in horror that she had been yelling—at an adult, no less! At some point during her outburst everyone had gathered around Captain Gunn and was staring at her, open-mouthed. Posy's eyes were as big as saucers. No one had ever heard Sophie yell before. Yes, she was an expert at scolding, and one of her sharp looks could intimidate the most unruly mischief-maker. But yell? Never.

"I mean, not that it's a terrible thing to be a cook," she said, suddenly feeling self-conscious and remembering Mrs. Baird and their own cook in Devon, who did this for a living and never complained. "I know you all enjoy my meals, and I am grateful that you help with the washing up. But, well...I mean...would it kill you all to give me a meal off now and then?"

Captain Gunn cleared his throat again. "We've been very thoughtless, Sophie. We took you for granted and gobbled up your excellent meals without considering all the time it took you to prepare them and how much you were missing out on."

"Yes, and we thought you liked cooking!" insisted Mark. He was a little worried about where his next meal would come from if Sophie went on strike. "You're so good at it!"

"Of course you can take a break," said Captain Gunn. "How about we make a schedule and let the others take a turn now and again?"

"Not sure how good I'll be at cooking, but I'm game to have a go," said Molly. "How about me and Leticia cook dinner tonight?"

Sophie grinned. "There's a challenge for an intrepid pirate! I won't have a leg to stand on if dinner is inedible!"

Everyone agreed that they had been selfish and assured Sophie of her value as an explorer as well as a cook. Soon the discussion turned back to their progress in hunting down Brother XII and, more importantly, the stolen gold.

"We just seem to be going from place to place without any solid evidence of where he ended up," bemoaned Molly. "I was looking for a real clue that would lead us right to him."

"Well, think of it this way," said Leticia. "If we can't figure out where he ended up, neither will anyone else. If it was easy, he would have been tracked down years ago and there wouldn't be any treasure to find!"

"I think it's a bit like one of those treasure hunts we used to have at birthday parties," said Harriet. "Each clue led you to the next, and at the end you found the prize. And in any case, aren't you all enjoying the cruise? It's really beautiful up here and just being on this boat is gorgeous."

Just then Captain Gunn glanced up and came face to face with a truly disreputable-looking character. He was tall and very thin, with a shock of black hair that hung around his face in matted ringlets. He had a gold ring in one ear, and they could see as he grinned at them that both his front teeth were missing. He stood on the dock with one dirty bare foot on the gunwale of *South Islander.*

"I'll thank you to remove your filthy foot from my boat," Captain Gunn said in a calm yet firm tone. "I don't think we have any business to conduct."

"Mebbe not," growled the man, scratching at his straggly beard, "but I hears you've been asking questions about Brother XII and wonder what you and a bunch of kids would want with him."

"Never you mind," said Molly. "Whatever we know we're keeping to ourselves."

"Ah, so you do knows something," said the man with an evil grin. "Thought you might. Well, don't you be thinking you can get away without us. We'll be watching."

And with that as a parting shot, he slouched off down the dock to join his motley crew on their boat, elegantly, but inappropriately, named *Black Pearl.*

"Here's what I think," said Captain Gunn. "I think we can outfox and outrun those men any day of the week, but it's going to take teamwork. How do you all feel about moving out in the middle of the night?"

"As long as Posy gets to bed at the proper time and stays there until morning," said Sophie.

As promised, Leticia and Molly cooked dinner. It wasn't as good as some of Sophie's meals, but for a campers' cookout, it was pretty tasty. Molly hauled a package of sausages out of the bottom of the freezer, and they cooked up a big pot of potatoes, which Leticia mashed with masses of butter and half a tin of evaporated milk. Molly fried up the sausages with a couple of onions and served it all with tinned baked beans. Sophie was not even allowed to do the washing up and was granted an evening free of domestic chores. The crew bedded down early, but were kept awake for a while by the shouting, singing, and carousing coming from the other boat. At last everything was quiet. But it seemed they had only been asleep for a few minutes when Captain Gunn went round the cabin shaking the crew awake.

"Those fellows are no doubt passed out, and it would take a fair bit to wake them, but we will keep absolute silence, just in case," he whispered. "Ian and Molly, I want you in the dinghy. You're going to tow us out. Mark, you can stand by for the engine when we are well away from the dock, and we'll get those sails up as soon as we can, even though there's precious little wind. Leticia and Harriet, you get ready to cast off the mooring lines, and Sophie, you take the wheel and steer where I point."

After their many adventures together, the crew were very good at working as a team, and soon *South Islander* was creeping away from the dock, heading for the entrance to the cove.

They were about fifty yards from the dock when Posy stuck her head out of the companionway, rubbing the sleep out of her eyes.

"Hey, what's going on?" she demanded in a piercing voice. "How come no one wakes me up when something exciting is going on? I'm not a baby anymore, you kn—"

"Ssssshh…" hissed Molly from the dinghy. "You'll wake the baddies."

It was too late. The crew watched in horror as someone stuck his head out of the hatch of the pirate's boat. The moonlight gleamed on the blond curls of the youngest of the Black Pearl's crew. Everyone froze, expecting the young pirate to yell for his captain and crewmates. Nothing happened. The children and the pirate stared at each other. Then, with a last glance at South Islander, the curly blond boy disappeared below.

"I think he's letting us go!" said Harriet in disbelief.

"Righto," said Captain Gunn. "Let's hope the rest of that crew are sunk into a drunken stupor and don't wake up. Quick, Molly and Ian, get to your oars and let's put some distance between them and us."

With Molly and Ian pulling at the oars in the dinghy, South Islander slipped silently through the water. As they pulled out into Lewis Channel, Mark started the engine, Ian and Molly climbed aboard out of the dinghy, and the whole crew hoisted all the sail they had. With a faint breeze and the engine ticking over, they headed across the channel.

"I want to get us tucked up out of sight as soon as possible, and definitely before daylight," said Captain Gunn. "The guidebook says Squirrel Cove is a very good anchorage, and I can only hope that once those fellows wake up, hopefully with very bad hangovers, they'll think we've headed north. Doesn't really make much sense for us to just cross the channel into Squirrel Cove, and since they're not very clever, I think they'll do what seems obvious to them—head north where rumour has it Brother XII may have gone to ground."

It took them less than an hour to cross Lewis Channel and head into Squirrel Cove between two small islands. They dropped the sails, and with the engine at its lowest speed, chugged quietly into the cove just as dawn was breaking. It was a magical place. Several small cabins dotted the shores, but once the crew penetrated deep into the back of the cove, the only things they could see were trees reflected in the still, calm water. They picked a spot, and the anchor rattled out through the hawser, momentarily breaking the utter quiet of the cove.

Nobody spoke. They just sat in the cockpit and absorbed the feeling of peace that descended on them. Finally, Harriet slipped down below and grabbed one of the books out of the boat's library.

"Captain Vancouver came in here when he was exploring in 1792 and stayed for a few days. He wrote about it in his journal and mentions what a special place it was. He also says that there are reversing falls that lead into a saltwater lagoon."

"What's a reversing fall?" said Posy, who had finally woken up and had poked her tousled head out of the companionway.

"I'm not sure," said Harriet. "Do you know, Captain Gunn?"

"Yes, I've seen a couple of examples of them on my travels. It means that at high tide the water flows from here into the lagoon, which is why it's salty, and at low tide the water pours out of the lagoon back into the cove. I think I can see them over there," he added, pointing to the far corner of the cove. "Grab those tide tables, Harriet, and we'll figure out what's the best time to take a ride down the falls."

Examining the tide tables, they reasoned that they could get a pretty good ride down from the lagoon back into the cove at around 6:00 p.m.

"We'll blow up that airbed that's stowed under the settee," said Captain Gunn. "You can carry it up the falls and ride back down."

After breakfast, the crew had been leaning back on the cushions in the cockpit and yawning after their early start.

"Everyone back into their bunks for a nap," ordered Sophie. "There's lots of time before the tide's right for the falls."

All the crew, with the exception of Captain Gunn, headed below and were soon fast asleep. Captain Gunn sat in the cockpit, puffing away at his pipe, looking at the charts, and having a good think about what they should do next. When the crew woke just in time for lunch, he called a meeting in the cockpit.

"I've had a look at the chart, and I think we can walk over to Von Donop Inlet where that farmer chappie lives. You remember the postmistress at Refuge Cove saying that he'd run into Brother xii a couple of years ago? I think we should go and take a look and see if we can see his cabin. If it looks promising we can sail around tomorrow."

The crew bent over the chart that Captain Gunn had spread on the table. They could see that Cortes Island had a narrow neck of land between Squirrel Cove and Von Donop Inlet that separated the two bodies of water by only a few hundred yards. One island was very nearly two islands, and it looked like they could cross over between Squirrel Cove and Von Donop Inlet without too much difficulty.

In actual fact it wasn't quite so easy. They rowed ashore to a point where there was a driftwood sign tacked onto a tree. "To Von Donop," it said, pointing into what looked like thick forest. There was a trail, but it was very faint and required a lot of climbing over fallen trees and whacking their way through some dense underbrush, but finally they found their way to the other side and ducked out from under the trees onto a sliver of muddy beach.

"Look!" cried Leticia, pointing to the other side of the inlet. "I can see something over there."

Sure enough, they could see the roof of a cabin set in a clearing surrounded by what looked like fruit trees.

"It would be good if we could hail the fellow that lives there and save ourselves a long sail around," said Captain Gunn. "Everyone yell 'Ahoy there' on the count of three. One, two, three..."

"AHOY THERE!" shouted captain and crew together, making a very impressive noise that echoed across the inlet. After three tries, they saw a figure emerge from the cabin and walk down to the shore. The crew jumped up and down and waved energetically, and finally the figure stepped into a small dinghy and headed across towards them.

"What's all that yelling about?" he demanded as he drew into the beach. "I came up here for a bit of peace and quiet, and what do I find but a whole gang of kids yelling at me! What do you want?"

The man stepped ashore and tied his dinghy to an overhanging branch. He was short, not much taller than Molly, and wore a huge beard that grew down to his chest. It was bright ginger and divided into three sections, each section plaited and tied with a shoelace. His hair was long, tied back with another shoelace, and he wore dungarees and a tattered pair of sneakers—missing their laces.

Captain Gunn explained their quest and wondered if he had anything to add to what they already knew. The fellow looked at the eager faces of the children, and after gazing out across the calm inlet for a few minutes, he seemed to come to a decision.

"I've had a few folks over the years ask about that man, but I didn't like the look of any of them, so I kept quiet. Not that I know much, but I will tell you that Brother xii—although I didn't know at the time that was who he was—did come in here a few years ago. He wanted to buy fruit and vegetables, and there was something about him that I just didn't like. Anyway, it was just me here, and I could see that his companion, a very strange-looking woman who had stayed in the boat, was holding a gun across her knees, so I decided not to argue. I sold him as little as I thought I could get away with, and they paid and headed out of the inlet. I was curious, so I followed, keeping one turn in the channel behind them, and when I got to the entrance of the inlet, I peeked around the corner and could see that they were heading north. A while later, when I went into Whaletown to pick up my mail, I heard stories about this man and his woman, Brother XII and Madame Z. If I were you I'd stay well away from them. They were bad news."

It didn't seem like much of a clue, but it was better than nothing. They were encountering people all along the coast who had either seen him in person or heard stories of him being in this area. The trail was not totally dead.

"If you're really that interested, I'd suggest you go into Whaletown and ask the folks in the post office. If anyone knows anything about anyone, it's them. Everyone for miles around picks up their mail there, and they get lots of people passing through on their way up and down the coast."

The crew thanked the man, and Sophie asked if he had any vegetables or fruit for sale. He took her and Leticia across the inlet, and when they came back half an hour later, they carried an old apple crate filled with an assortment of delicious fresh produce. Captain Gunn paid him, and they parted the best of friends before the crew headed back into the forest for the walk back to Squirrel Cove.

AFTER AN EARLY dinner of pork chops, fried potatoes, and salad made from the vegetables they had bought earlier, the crew, clad in their swimming gear, squeezed into the dinghy and rowed over to the bottom of the falls with the airbed balanced across the gunwales. The falls weren't really falls, just what looked like a steep creek bed at the top of which they could see the edge of the lagoon. They landed the dinghy and tied it to a tree, attached a line to the airbed, and scrambled up the creek towing the airbed behind them. The creek bed was fairly smooth, and it looked as if the airbed could make it down without being punctured on sharp rocks. Ian and Molly tried it first. They slid down the falls and shot out into the cove, where they promptly tipped over. Soon all of them—except Posy, who wasn't a very good swimmer—had taken turns shooting the rapids and swimming back to shore from the airbed, which had a tendency to flip as soon as they reached the bottom. It was great fun, but eventually they noticed that the level of the cove was rising, and the run was getting shorter and shorter as the tide came in.

They headed back to *South Islander* where they all towelled off and put on their pyjamas. The wet bathing suits were pegged out on the lifelines and Leticia prepared hot chocolate for everyone. As they were sitting in the cockpit with their steaming mugs, they noticed a canoe approaching the boat. It was a beautiful craft with a carved prow and it was adorned with painted designs of various creatures. Paddling it were two Native men, with a Native woman sitting amidships cradling a baby.

The canoe came alongside *South Islander.*

"Have you seen an old boat with a bunch of drunks onboard?" asked the older of the two men. "We think they're the ones who ruined our nets and stole our catch a few weeks ago. We heard they were back in the area."

"Oh, we know them all right. They were over in Refuge Cove, and they're trying to follow us. That's why we are tucked up in here," said Molly. "We're hoping to sneak out of here and head north round the top of Cortes and down to Whaletown tomorrow."

"Well, we'll be on the lookout for them. And if we do run into them and they ask about a boat full of kids and an old man"—Captain Gunn looked askance at being described this way—"we'll tell them you went the other way."

"Thank you very much," said Harriet. "Would you like some hot chocolate before you go?"

This offer was declined, but the men were happy with the "old man's" gift of pipe tobacco, and Sophie wrapped up some of her latest loaf of bread spread with butter and honey and gave it to the woman, who accepted it with a shy smile.

The canoe headed back across the cove, and the crew were soon heading below to bed, exhausted by their early start, long walk, and fun at the falls.

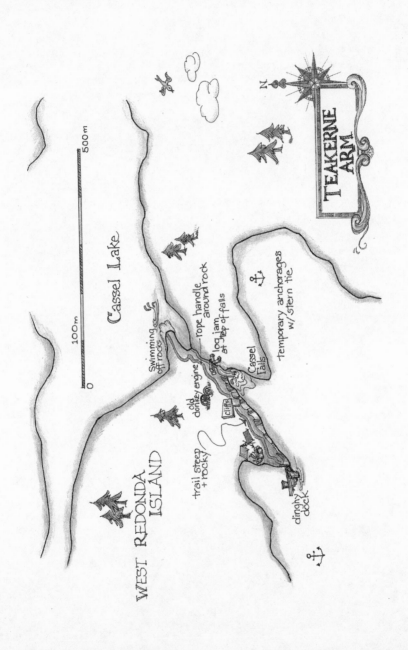

WEST REDONDA ISLAND

Cassel Lake

500m
100m
0

Swimming off rocks

rope handle around rock

log jam at top of falls

old donkey engine

trail steep + rocky

Cassel Falls

cliff

temporary anchorages w/ stern tie

dinghy dock

TEAKERNE ARM

N

CHAPTER SEVEN

A DAY OFF FROM TREASURE HUNTING

"**I** KNOW WE WANT to find the treasure," said Captain Gunn, "but don't forget this is supposed to be a holiday too. I would like to see this waterfall in Teakerne Arm that's marked on the chart, and Sophie might be interested in the freshwater lake. You can all take proper baths and do some laundry. No handy Mr. Chen with his Chinese laundry up here."

They were just about ready to leave Squirrel Cove. Molly wanted to head straight up and round the northern tip of Cortes Island so that they could get down to Whaletown on the other side of the island and follow up on possible clues. The others agreed with Captain Gunn. The waterfall and lake sounded like fun. Molly gave in.

"All right," she said, "but we have to be jolly careful not to run into the baddies. For all we know they might be leaving Refuge Cove just as we come out of here, and then we'd have a hard time shaking them off."

"It's still early," replied Captain Gunn, "and I'm pretty sure they are a hard-drinking lot who don't get up with the larks like we do. If we get going now, and if we send Ian and Molly ahead in the dinghy to scout out Lewis Channel, I think we can make the dash across and up into Teakerne Arm. If they do cross over to Squirrel Cove later we know our friends will send them the wrong way."

And that's what they did. After coming out of the inner cove and before they were in straight line of sight to the entrance to Refuge Cove across Lewis Channel, Ian and Molly took the dinghy and the telescope and rowed ahead. They scanned the channel and then signalled *South Islander* that it was clear to move forward. They were soon on-board again and headed out into the channel.

"Mark, we need full steam ahead," said Captain Gunn.

Mark was only too keen to get to work. Soon the engine was throbbing hard and the boat was moving swiftly across the channel. Everyone watched anxiously just in case the other boat was coming out of Refuge Cove, but they saw nothing. A little while later they were out of sight in Teakerne Arm, heading deep into the inlet towards the waterfall and lake.

AS THEY NEARED the head of the inlet, they could see the waterfall cascading over a cliff into a tiny cove. Tied to the shore nearby was a huge raft of logs. As they watched, a couple more logs tumbled over the waterfall and bobbed around the cove.

Anchoring was a bit of a challenge because the steep walls on the shore plunged straight down and deep into the water, and they had to let out fathoms and fathoms of chain before the anchor took hold.

"I think we'd better stern-tie here," said Captain Gunn.

Ian rowed ashore with the end of a long line and put it round a tree poking out of the rocks. He brought the free end back to the boat and soon they were snugly attached fore and aft, with the stern a mere three yards away from the shore.

A steep trail took them up beside a rocky cliff. From the top they got a bird's-eye view of the waterfall plunging into the cove below. The very top of the cliff was a rocky plateau, and they could see various items of machinery from it as well as loops of steel cable that appeared to be part of some logging operation. As they followed the creek from the top of the waterfall they heard the buzzing sound of saws, and at the outlet from the lake to the creek they came across two men trimming logs and getting ready to send them over the waterfall and into the inlet.

"Hello there," said one of the men, who wore the most splendid pair of bright red suspenders, a checkered shirt, blue jeans, and enormous boots. "Don't see many folks up this far. Nice boat you've got. I watched you coming in."

They stood and chatted with the loggers and discovered that the men would be gathering logs for another week, at which time a tug would come in and pick them up along with their log boom.

The lake was a couple of hundred yards farther along the trail, which ended on a bare slope of rock that led straight down into the crystal clear water. The children wasted no time changing into their bathing suits and scrambling down into the lake. Posy was equipped with an inflatable rubber ring and joined the others, carefully supervised by Sophie. The water was warm and felt silky on their skin, and Sophie ordered everyone to get their hair wet and shampoo with the bottle she had brought along. As the crew toasted on the warm rocks, Sophie and Leticia prepared to do the laundry. Suddenly Sophie put down the large bar of soap she'd brought along and whispered in Leticia's ear. Leticia grinned.

"We're going on strike," she said to the recumbent crew lazing on the rocks. "Sophie's been reading about something called women's rights, and we think it's time to put it into practice."

Captain Gunn grinned. Ever since Sophie's outburst over the cooking, he'd noticed a change in her. She was less bound by rules and regulations, was participating more in the planning of their adventure, and generally seemed to be enjoying herself. And now women's rights! He liked seeing this rebellious streak in her.

"I think they mean that the men should take a turn at doing the laundry," he explained, seeing Mark's and Ian's confused faces. "Right, boys, jump to it! Ian, you scrub with the soap. Mark, you give everything a good rinse, and I'll wring."

The girls watched in delight as for the next hour the men struggled with the laundry. It didn't exactly meet Sophie's high standards, but still, this was a small victory—hopefully one of many yet to come.

LATER THAT DAY the whole crew descended the trail back to the boat. Soon the lifelines were draped with laundry and the crew hauled in the anchor, untied the stern line, and motored out towards Lewis Channel.

As they approached the entrance to the channel, Captain Gunn ordered Mark to put the engine to idle, and they crept slowly out into open water, with Molly at the end of the bowsprit with the telescope. Just as they came out in the open, she pointed wildly to port. The others could just see the stern of a large boat disappearing into the distance, down the eastern shore of Cortes Island. They couldn't be sure, but it seemed likely the boat belonged to the men that had been following them. The crew's Native friends had done what they had promised and sent the men off on a wild goose chase.

It was a long sail, but eventually they passed the northernmost tip of Cortes Island and started heading south down the western shore. They passed the entrance to Von Donop Inlet, and just as it was beginning to get dark they reached Whaletown, where they found a spot on the government dock.

THE NEXT MORNING the entire crew was waiting impatiently outside the post office. As soon as it opened on the dot of 9:00 a.m. they all crowded inside to talk to the postmistress.

Obviously tending a post office gave one an exceptional grasp of local affairs. Everyone came in at one time or another to pick up mail and gossip. This doughty lady was no exception. As soon as they mentioned Brother XII she wouldn't stop talking.

"Nasty piece of work he was," she started. "Made us all feel real uncomfortable when he came in. He didn't come in often, but we saw him a few times. Never wanted to engage in conversation and just told us to mind our own business if we asked any questions. That woman he had with him was almost worse. Saw her a few times trying to chat up some of our local young women. They'd been warned, though, and knew enough to turn their backs. Anyway, the visits stopped a year or so ago, and we've heard neither hide nor hair about them since. What did you say your names were?" she added. "I got some mail addressed to the crew of the *South Islander*, c/o Captain Gunn. Would that happen to be you lot?"

"Yes," said Molly eagerly. "What do you have for us?"

The woman brought out a bundle of letters from under the counter and handed it over.

"Oh, look," said Sophie. "Letters from home. I wonder how they knew to send them here."

"I gave Wei Chen's address to your parents and asked him to forward mail here. I'd had a good look at the chart and figured we'd be poking our noses in here sooner or later. Wanted it to be a surprise for you lot to get letters from home."

And a very pleasant surprise it was. As well as letters from both mothers in England, there was one from Commander Phillips, posted before his ship left Montreal. The last letter in the pile was one no one recognized. It had a Canadian stamp, and they didn't know anyone in Canada who would be writing to them.

Captain Gunn opened it, scanned it briefly, and then turned to the children.

"This one's from our friend Jasper Peabody," he said. "It seems he forgot to tell us something that he thinks might be helpful. Apparently, Brother xii had a cousin who was a priest up in a place called Church House. It's not far from here. Past the north end of Cortes and over on the mainland. Jasper thinks we should go and talk to him. Not a bad idea, though we would be retracing our steps a bit."

"Let's go," said Molly. "Any clue is better than just cruising around hoping Brother xii will just pop up from behind a rock and hand us the treasure!"

"I want to post a letter back to Mother before we go," said Sophie.

"What about sending postcards to everyone?" suggested Harriet. "Look! They have some nice ones of Desolation Sound."

"I'm going to send the one I saw of the grizzly bear," said Mark. "I just wish we could see one in real life."

Cards were chosen, written, and signed by the appropriate children. They watched as the postmistress stuck on Canadian stamps and postmarked the cards before tossing them into a sack.

"Funny to think of the journey they will have to make before they get to Mother and Father," said Sophie. "By the time they get them we may have found the treasure!"

"Not *may* have—*will* have!" said Molly. "Of course we're going to find it, but we won't find it standing around here, so let's get going!"

Half an hour later *South Islander* was again heading north, backtracking to the tip of Cortes Island. The vista of mountains was getting more and more impressive the farther north they went, and the shorelines of islands and mainland seemed to rear straight up out of the water. It was a gorgeous day, sunny and hot, with not a breath of wind. Mark was tending the engine and the others were lolling around on deck, soaking up the sun.

"Everyone needs to wear their sun hats," Sophie reminded them. "We don't want anyone getting sunstroke." Sometimes Sophie seemed to be the only adult on-board, especially as Captain Gunn often behaved like an overgrown schoolboy.

"How about some fishing?" said the overgrown schoolboy. "I know all the tackle is on-board in one of the cockpit lockers. You can catch some jolly big salmon in these waters. Not the same as Scottish salmon—but much, much better, so I've heard."

It took a while, but eventually and with the help of the fishing book they found in the boat's library, the fishing gear was rigged and they slowed the engine so that they were moving slowly through the water.

"No point in speeding along. Won't catch any fish that way, according to this book. We need to go slowly and hope that the salmon are attracted to the spinner we've got down there."

Going slowly, especially on a treasure hunt, was not on Molly's agenda, but she conceded more or less gracefully and her patience was rewarded about half an hour later when they got a bite.

"Ian, you reel him in," said Captain Gunn. "Nice and slowly, and if he makes a run for it let the line out and then reel it back in again. One of you others get ready with the net."

It was all accomplished in textbook fashion, and soon there was a salmon, which had been humanely dispatched with an oar, lying in the cockpit.

"What do you think it weighs?" asked Mark. "Ten pounds?" he added hopefully.

Captain Gunn laughed. "Typical fisherman, exaggerating his catch, although it was really Ian's catch. I'd say three or four pounds. Enough for a slap-up dinner. Do you think you can cook it, Sophie?"

"Well, I've never tried fresh salmon, though I've made fish cakes with the tinned stuff," she replied.

"This is way too good for fish cakes," laughed Captain Gunn. "We've got a couple of lemons. Try baking it in the oven with butter and lemon."

As soon as they had landed the fish, they had put the engine into full speed ahead, and were now skirting some small islands, with the bulk of the mainland rising to their starboard. Everyone had had a good look at the chart. Captain Gunn insisted that the whole crew, Posy included, study the chart as they went.

"Church House isn't far ahead," said Leticia. "Over there, round the next point."

As they rounded the point, ready to head into the dock they could see ahead, the whole crew gasped in horror. Heading out from the dock was Black Pearl. "They must have realized we had gone the other way and passed us while we were holed up in Whaletown," said Molly as she grabbed the telescope and observed the motley crew lounging on the deck of the run-down boat.

The Black Pearl passed them, coming within a few hundred yards of South Islander. They were near enough to hear the jeering and catcalls directed at them.

"Bad luck, you miserable kids!" shouted one of them, the one who had approached them at Refuge Cove. "We're going to find that gold, and you don't stand a chance. Better go home to jolly old England before someone gets hurt. And don't think you can follow us—if you do, you'll get a taste of this." He brandished a shotgun in their direction.

There didn't seem to be anything else to do but proceed to the dock. They tied up, tidied the boat—something Captain Gunn always insisted on before heading ashore—and walked up the dock towards the white church they could see nearby. The shore was lined with cabins, and there were totem poles along the gravel road that ran parallel with the shore.

"We had better get permission from the chief before we start waltzing around as if we owned the place. This is their territory, and we should all be very respectful of it," said Captain Gunn.

A group of small children watched them silently. Captain Gunn asked them if they knew where he could find the chief, and one of them ran off into the largest of the cabins. A short time later a very old man emerged from the cabin and came to meet them.

"We don't get many visitors, and you're the second group today," he said as he approached the crew. "We didn't much like the others, but I couldn't get rid of them until they'd spoken to Father Wilson. I'm wondering if you are after the same thing they were."

"Probably," said Captain Gunn, "but I'd like to think we have better motives than that bunch of villains. And, yes, we'd like to talk to Father Wilson if it's all right with you."

"Go right ahead," replied the chief. "You'll find him in the rectory, just behind the church."

Sure enough, in the white painted cottage that served as the rectory, they found Father Wilson and explained their quest.

"That last lot of visitors shook me up," he said as he sipped at a glass full of what looked suspiciously like whisky. "They came in here on a hunch apparently, because it's one of the only settlements around. I'm afraid I let on that Brother XII was my cousin. I was getting flustered because they were looking very aggressive, and I thought I could get rid of them if I told them everything I know, which isn't much."

"Can you tell us what you do know?" asked Molly. "We've been following the trail, but really all we know is that he might have ended up somewhere near here."

"All I know is that he came to visit with that dreadful woman of his. We grew up together in England; our fathers were brothers, but he was always the odd man out and became more peculiar as he got older. He disappeared years ago, and this was the first time I'd seen him for ages. Odd coincidence that we should both end up in British Columbia. Anyway, he started asking me if there was any land for sale that was remote and where it would be hard to track him down. I didn't ask him why anyone would be wanting to track him down, but I'd heard the stories of what he'd been up to and I'm not surprised he wanted to disappear. Well, it's all pretty remote around here, but not much land that can support a settlement. Mostly raw forest and very, very hard work to clear enough for farming. I told him I'd heard of a piece for sale on the other side of Sonora Island at a place called Owen Bay. There was a bit of a settlement there, but mostly loners who wouldn't bother him. I heard later that he had bought a cabin in Owen Bay, but I never saw him again. I told those other men what I knew, so I suppose that's where they are heading, but if you ask me, Edward is long gone."

They left Father Wilson sitting at his kitchen table, musing on the strangeness of life. How did two people so closely related end up so very different from each other? One dedicated his life to God and moved halfway around the world to try to make life better for those less fortunate than him. The other believed he *was* God and put his efforts into making others believe this, all for his own personal gain. There was no explanation, and eventually Father Wilson sighed, put away the whisky bottle, and went back to work.

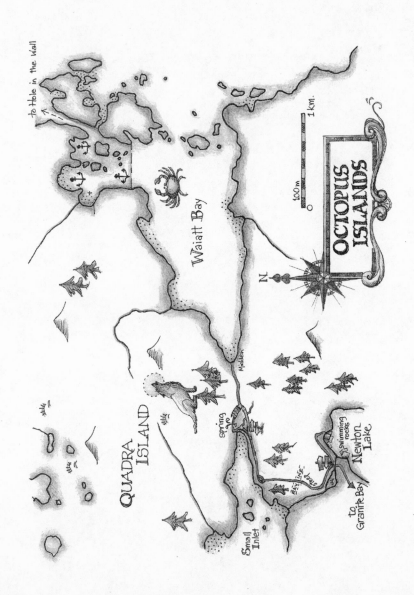

to Hole in the Wall

OCTOPUS ISLANDS

1 km.

100 m

N

Waiatt Bay

QUADRA ISLAND

Midden

Spring

Small Inlet

Newton Lake

Swimming rocks

to Granite Bay

Small Inlet trail

CHAPTER EIGHT
INTO THE HOLE

A SHORT TIME LATER, *South Islander* pulled away from Church House and headed for the entrance to Hole in the Wall, the narrow passage between Maurelle and Sonora Islands, which ended in a set of fearsome tidal rapids. Ian and Leticia were studying the tide and current tables.

"They'd better not be thinking of going through that gap now," said Leticia. "It's at maximum flood in about half an hour. They'll never get through with the tide running against them at eleven knots."

As they entered the channel leading towards the Hole, Molly, who was up on the end of the bowsprit, gave a shout.

"I can see them—they're heading straight for the Hole!"

The current in the main part of the channel was minimal, and they were catching up with the other boat, which was approaching the tiny gap at the end and being slowed down by the tremendous tide flowing against it. It was like trying to paddle a canoe up a waterfall. Captain Gunn steered *South Islander* over to a small nook on the shore of Maurelle Island and ordered Molly to get off the bowsprit and help Ian with the anchor.

"No matter what, there's no way we're going through there for at least another five hours," said Captain Gunn. "That's the next slack water. Jolly dangerous to attempt that gap even when you have the current going with you. If your engine fails—yes, Mark, I know that's very unlikely with you in charge—but if it *does* fail, you have no steerage and your boat can be swirled around in the whirlpools. It's actually more dangerous going with the current than trying to go against it. Full flood, and the water is ripping and whirling around in there just waiting to catch a foolish boater in its jaws."

They all crowded up to the foredeck and took turns watching the *Black Pearl* through the telescope as it approached the narrowest part of the channel. And then it happened.

The boat seemed to falter, and then instead of heading straight for the gap it started rotating, slowly at first and then faster and faster as it was caught in the current. It wasn't clear if the engine had failed, but they were totally out of control, and in seconds there was a thunderous crash and the *Pearl* hit the rocks on the Maurelle Island side of the channel. Everything seemed to happen in slow motion. For a minute it looked like the boat would slide off the rocks and be whirled around in the tremendous current and then swept back along the channel towards *South Islander*, but then it seemed to leap forwards on the rocks with a dreadful tearing sound. The crew of the *Black Pearl* was running up and down the decks yelling madly, and then with one accord they abandoned ship, leaping off the bow as it slid backwards and forwards off and on the rocks. The crew of *South Islander* watched in horror as one of the villains missed the jump and was very nearly swept off the rocks into the swirling waters. What made it worse was that it was the young blond pirate who had let them go in Refuge Cove. Fortunately one of his shipmates was able to grab him and drag him up over the slippery rocks, and eventually the whole crew was on the shore, jumping up and down and swearing. With a groan, the Black Pearl lurched forwards and ground to a halt, ending up lying sideways on the rocks.

"Shouldn't we go and help them?" asked Sophie. Her words came out muffled as she had her hands clamped over her mouth in shock.

"Absolutely not," replied Captain Gunn. "They all made it to shore and they'll come to no harm there. It is much too dangerous to reach them now, and even if the water was dead calm, they're a nasty lot and I don't want them anywhere near you. We'll wait here until slack and then go through. I hope they won't be waiting to take a potshot at us."

Molly's eyes gleamed. "Imagine getting shot at! What a great story to tell when we get home."

"No one's getting shot at," said Captain Gunn. "I'd never be brave enough to face your mothers if I came home with fewer children than I started out with."

And so they waited. There didn't seem to be much else to do, so Sophie got to work preparing the salmon. A while later they were all sitting round the cockpit enjoying the meal. Fresh salmon lathered with butter and lemon juice and baked in the oven (they all agreed it was the best fish they'd ever tasted), boiled potatoes, and fresh peas from their gardener friend in Von

Donop. Dessert was bananas and custard, and by the time the meal was over they could hardly move. Captain Gunn enjoyed his with a glass of wine, while the others drank lemonade.

FINALLY THE CLOCK showed that slack tide was only half an hour away.

"We'll leave now, and by the time we get there it should be totally slack. If the tide turns a few minutes sooner, we'll have the first of the ebb to help us through," said Captain Gunn. "It should only be running at two or three knots against us by now, and all the whirlpools will have calmed down. Safe to go, but I want all of you below in case any of those fellows gets trigger-happy."

Molly was about to argue but caught Sophie's eye and thought better of it. She and Ian raised the anchor, Mark had the engine ticking over, and they approached the end of the channel. The crew headed down below, leaving Captain Gunn at the wheel. Hole in the Wall was truly a very narrow gap, and the shore where the Black Pearl rested was a mere six yards away. The children peered through the portholes as they slipped past the wreck, but it seemed the crew of the grounded boat had disappeared.

"You can come out now," said Captain Gunn. "No sign of those villains. Seems they've decided to go for a hike. Looking for a lift off the island, no doubt, but I don't think they'll have much luck. I don't think anyone lives on Maurelle Island. Looking at the state of their boat, they won't get her off those rocks anytime soon, especially as the tide is dropping now. No, I think it's pretty safe to say we've seen the last of that lot for a while."

On the other side of Hole in the Wall, the crew of *South Islander* found themselves in a wide channel, with islands ahead of them and the channel stretching north and south.

"As it's near slack now and the ebb tide could take us up into Owen Bay, we could keep going, but I think we should take a break and stay over in these Octopus Islands I see on the chart. With those madmen out of the way, there's no hurry and it would be a shame to miss this spot. It's pretty gorgeous and also there is a good crabbing spot. I've been dying to try the crab pot we have on-board."

There were more rolled eyes from Molly, but the others were happy to do some exploring. Their previous adventures had all been in places where there was at least a modicum of civilization not too far away, but this was pristine wilderness and not much else.

South Islander wound its way through the narrow channels and between the small islands that made up the little archipelago of the Octopus Islands. They came out into a small bay surrounded by islands, went through the now well-practised routine of anchoring, and were engulfed in the absolute quiet of their surroundings.

It was getting late, but the sun was still up and the air was warm. Captain Gunn dug out the crab trap from one of the lockers and rigged it with a long line and a spare float.

"Sophie, can you spare a chicken leg from that packet of frozen ones that we got from Wei Chen?" he shouted down the companionway, where Sophie and Leticia were tidying up.

Sophie pulled everything out of the cooler, and found the chicken legs. They had partially thawed, and she was able to pry them apart, handing one up to Captain Gunn on deck. He tied the piece of meat inside the trap, checked everything was secure, and lowered it into the dinghy that Ian and Molly had pulled alongside.

"Row right out into the middle of the large bay over there," he said, pointing them in the right direction. "Just throw it overboard—the float will mark the spot so we can haul it up tomorrow."

On the way back from the designated spot, Ian and Molly rowed around some of the tiny islands and scoped out an excellent swimming spot with flat rocks sloping down into the water.

"It's too late this evening, but I'll race you from the boat to this spot first thing in the morning," said Molly as they pulled in beside their mother ship.

"Everyone hit their bunks," said Captain Gunn. "We've got another exciting day tomorrow, and who knows, this might be the day we catch up with our pet villain!"

AT SOME POINT during the night, every member of the crew (except Posy, who slept right through without waking) had woken up and listened to the distant howling of wolves. They were safe and snug on *South Islander*, but somewhere not too far away on Quadra Island, wild wolves roamed free and howled to the moon. They were adventurers, explorers, and pirates in an untamed wilderness—about as far from the tame English countryside as it was possible to be.

Early the next morning the crew were awakened by a terrific shriek and a loud splash as Molly leapt off the gunwales into the water. One splash was quickly followed by another as Ian dove neatly in after her and almost instantly came up spluttering and thrashing.

"It's freezing," he gasped, before speeding off at a skilful crawl after Molly, who was already heading for the island they had scoped out the night before. The rest of the crew, still clad in their pyjamas, lined the rail and started cheering them on.

"Go, Molly, go!" yelled her fellow pirate, sister, and shipmate, Leticia. "You can beat him!"

Ian had a larger cheering team as his three sisters started yelling their support. Captain Gunn, to even things up, teamed up with Leticia and Mark to cheer on Molly.

It was a very close race, but Ian had been part of his swimming team last term and beat Molly by a length to the island. They both climbed out and started jumping up and down in an attempt to warm up.

"Let's go and pick them up in the dinghy," said Sophie. "We don't want them catching cold."

Sophie and Leticia, with Posy wedged in the bow, rowed ashore and picked up the shivering racers, greeting them with backslaps and dry towels.

"I'm going to make a big pot of porridge," said Sophie. "It'll warm them up and be a good start to the day."

"Why is the water so cold here and it's supposed to be so warm on Savary Island?" asked Molly a little while later as they sat round the cockpit table tucking into steaming bowls of porridge liberally sprinkled with sugar and doused in evaporated milk from their stock of tins. She had finally stopped shivering and was now warmly wrapped in a thick sweater with her red knitted cap pulled firmly over her wet hair.

Captain Gunn took a sheet of paper and a pencil and started drawing.

"This lump here is Vancouver Island," he said as he sketched a rough map. "The tide doesn't just flow north and south as the tide ebbs and flows. See my arrows? The tides flood in from both ends of the island and ebb back the way they came. So where we are now, the ebb flows north and the tide floods south. Once you get below Quadra Island, it's the opposite. You need to look at the chart carefully because it's not as if there's a straight line above where the tide goes one way, and below where the tide goes the other. It's a very rough line, but Savary Island is right around the point where the tides meet. So there's very little tidal exchange and the water gets a chance to warm up. Not to mention that the waters off Savary are pretty shallow and heat up quickly once the weather is hot and sunny. Now here we are right smack in the middle of a trio of tidal rapids, Hole in the Wall, Okisollo Rapids—that's where we're going through today—and Surge Narrows down south at the end of this channel. With all that water rushing in and out it's no wonder the water is freezing."

"Well, I'm going to save my swimming for when we get to Savary," said Leticia.

CAPTAIN GUNN AND Ian had studied the current tables very carefully to decide the exact time they should negotiate the Upper Rapids in Okisollo Channel. The chart had a notation that clearly stated: "Overfalls and eddies in the upper rapids are extremely dangerous." No one was going to argue with that statement, so they checked and rechecked the tables.

"It's slack water at 1:20 this afternoon," said Captain Gunn, "and then it turns to ebb, which means we'll have the current going with us to the entrance to Owen Bay. We'll up anchor at 1:00, which will give us twenty minutes to get back through these islands and get ready to head north through the rapids. It will be completely slack as we start and then we'll get a little bit of current going with us—nothing to worry about. It's all in the timing. We certainly don't want to be idiots like that other lot on *Black Pearl*."

While they waited, Molly, Leticia, Ian, and Sophie rowed in the dinghy out to the crab trap. They quickly spotted the orange float, brought it aboard, and hauled in the line. It was a very long line, so it took a while to get to the end that was attached to the trap, but eventually they could see it rising up through the clear water. They had definitely caught something.

"Golly," exclaimed Leticia. "We've landed a trapful!"

When they finally had the trap resting on the forward thwart, they could see that they had five snapping crustaceans eyeing them balefully from between the bars of the trap.

"I've brought a tape measure," said Ian. "Captain Gunn told me we have to throw back anything less than six inches across the shell, and we have to throw back all females."

"Good luck measuring them," laughed Molly as she surveyed the waving pincers that filled the trap.

They managed to extricate the crabs one by one into the bottom of the dinghy, and after much discussion and comparison with the sketch of male and female crabs that Captain Gunn had given Ian, they decided they could keep the three largest. They threw back the other two, put the ones they were keeping into a bucket of salt water, and headed back to *South Islander*. The bucket of crabs was covered with a towel and placed in a corner of the deck while Sophie and Leticia flipped through the on-board cookbooks to find the best way to prepare them.

"We'll leave the killing and cleaning to Captain Gunn," said Leticia. "There's no way I'm going to do it."

"Well, that seems to be the only tricky bit," replied Sophie. "After we get them cut in half, all we have to do is boil them in plenty of salted water for about ten minutes. Then they're ready to eat with loads of melted butter and lemon juice. I don't think we have enough for a full meal for all of us, but they'll make a nice starter, and we can have something simple for our main course."

They had a quick lunch with their new favourite food— peanut butter, which was completely unheard of in England.

They spread a thick layer of the stuff on Sophie's homemade bread, topped it off with honey and bananas, and accompanied this gourmet delight with steaming mugs of tea.

"I'm going to pack my suitcase full of peanut butter when we go home," declared Mark.

Everyone laughed at the thought of Mark dragging his duffel bag filled with clinking jars of peanut butter all the way back to England.

As the time of slack water approached, the crew got ready to leave once again. Leticia and Sophie took a turn at raising the anchor between them, Mark started the engine and put it into gear, and they slipped back through the islands until they were out in the main channel. They could clearly see the wreck of the Black Pearl on the rocks beside Hole in the Wall, but there was still no sign of its crew.

"Perhaps someone picked them up and they are gone forever," said Leticia.

"Could be," replied Captain Gunn. "But more likely they've hiked over to the other side of the island hoping to hail a passing boat. Not much traffic through here. They'll have a long and difficult walk whichever way they decide to go. You can see it's mostly forest and rock and pretty steep too."

The crew gazed up and down the channel. There was not a single other boat in sight. It gave them an uneasy feeling to know that if they got into trouble it might be a very long time before anyone came along to help.

Captain Gunn turned the boat to port, carefully checking the chart before heading into the Upper Rapids, which at slack water showed no sign of the eddies and overfalls the chart had warned about. They proceeded along the channel, with Quadra Island on their port side and Sonora Island on their starboard side. Once they had passed the rapids they turned into Owen Bay between a small island and an outcrop of land.

The bay was large and completely calm. As they came round the end of the small island on their starboard side, they saw the dock tucked into the southernmost corner of the bay. They motored slowly over to the dock, which was devoid of any sign of life, put the fenders over, prepared the mooring lines, and— with Ian jumping off with the bow line and Molly with the stern line—were soon secured.

Surely this would be the place where they finally caught up with Brother XII and the fabled treasure.

CHAPTER NINE
THE END OF THE TRAIL

AN HOUR LATER the crew had explored everything there was to explore and were back at the boat. There had been a few tumbledown cabins in a clearing at the top of the dock, but not much else. The whole place had a gloomy, neglected feel about it.

"How are we ever going to find out where Brother XII lived?" asked Leticia. "There doesn't seem to be any sign of anybody, never mind him."

"Nothing much to see around here," agreed Captain Gunn. "I think we should put a search party in the dinghy and take a good look round the bay."

They decided that Ian, Molly, Leticia, Harriet, and Posy would go in the dinghy and row round the bay looking for any signs of life. Mark said he had work to do on the engine, and Sophie was busy planning and preparing dinner—cheerfully this time, as she'd had a break from it for the past couple of nights. Captain Gunn announced he was going to take a nice long nap.

The dinghy crew set off from the dock and began a shoreline search of the bay. It was a big bay, and progress was slow as they kept going into shore to check out things that looked interesting. As they neared the head of the bay, they noticed a deep indentation in the shoreline and pulled the dinghy in closer to investigate. There were some loose logs floating around in a little cove and the remains of a small dock. It looked hopeful, so they brought the dinghy into a tiny beach, tied it to an overhanging branch, and stepped ashore. They soon discovered that there was a small stream that flowed into the cove with some tumbledown buildings set beside the stream, just a few feet back from the cove. The children looked around carefully, and then Leticia gave a shout.

"I think there's a path that goes up beside the stream. Let's see where it goes."

It was a narrow but easy-to-follow trail, and it ran mostly alongside the stream on their left.

"What's that?" asked Posy, pointing to a long, narrow wooden structure that was built right into the stream bed.

"I think it might have something to do with logging," replied Ian, "but I'm not sure exactly how it works. In any case, it looks pretty rundown. I don't think it's been used recently."

The structure resembled the train trestles they had glimpsed while travelling through the mountains. Built with crossed timbers, the top appeared to contain some sort of trough that may have had water running down it at one time, though it was now completely dry.

After about half an hour of gradual climbing, the trail abruptly opened out, and they found themselves on the shores of a lake. The lake was surrounded by trees, and the edges appeared to be marshy. Close to where the stream exited the lake heading down to the bay, they saw more logs jammed up against the shore.

"Doesn't seem much to see here," said Leticia. "I think we should be heading back. We don't want to be late for Sophie's crab dinner."

They turned away from the lake and trekked back down the trail. At the very bottom, hidden in the forest (they had missed it on their way up), they came across another wooden building. This one was in better condition than the tumbledown ones by the cove. It resembled nothing more or less than a tool shed, and in fact, when they opened the door they found some broken and rusty tools left behind by whoever had been living and working there.

The somewhat dispirited crew boarded the dinghy and rowed back to *South Islander*, where a cloud of steam was spiralling out of the companionway. Soon they were all sitting round the table, each with a crab leg on their plate and everyone wondering what to do next.

"You have to crack the shell to get at the meat," said Captain Gunn. "Here, try these."

He passed around a pair of pliers from the boat's tool kit, and everyone had a turn cracking their leg and then prying out the sweet meat. Sophie had melted a pan of butter and sliced a lemon, and the crew dipped and squeezed and declared crab a very tasty treat, even though it took a lot of work to produce each forkful. When the crab was finished, Sophie produced a huge pan of her famous scrambled eggs, which they ate with big slabs of bread and butter and a salad from their Von Donop friend's garden.

"I think we have to accept that we've had a great adventure, but we aren't going to find that treasure," said Captain Gunn as he leaned back in a corner of the cockpit and lit his pipe. "We've had a good cruise so far, but we need to start heading back down south. I don't want to rush, and we've missed some good anchorages in our hurry to track Brother XII."

"You can't really be thinking of giving up," said Molly, jumping up and hitting her head on the boom. "Ouch! Come on, all of you! We are on the trail, and we *must* be getting close."

"I think we've followed all the clues there are," said Leticia, "and we seem to have reached a dead end. We still have a great story to tell when we get home, and Uncle Bert has got lots of material for two more books. If he gets going writing them we can have another great holiday next year."

"Thanks a lot," laughed Captain Gunn. "All I'm good for is making lots of money on my books so I can take you ungrateful lot on holiday.

"All right, all right," he said as Molly opened her mouth to protest, "I didn't mean it like that. You are all very good company and adventuring by myself wouldn't be half as much fun."

The clean-up crew got to work, and when they had finished and the galley and cockpit were shipshape, Leticia made a big saucepan of cocoa. The evening was chilly, so they wrapped themselves up in sweaters and talked over what they knew and what they still didn't know.

"We know for certain that Brother XII visited his cousin at Church House, and we're pretty sure he ended up here in Owen Bay, but there aren't any clues to lead us to him or the treasure," said Ian. "I think Captain Gunn is right and we should chalk this up to a tremendous adventure and really enjoy our cruise back down to Vancouver."

"You must be joking!" exclaimed Molly, jumping up again and almost spilling her cocoa. "We are so close. I mean, we actually know for a fact that he visited here, and it seems likely that he settled here. No one heard anything about him after this, so it's a pretty good bet that the story of Brother XII ends in Owen Bay. We have to keep looking!"

"But Captain Gunn has a point," said Sophie. "There is so much more to see, and it would be a shame to hang about in this place, find nothing, and then have to hotfoot it back to Vancouver, missing some gorgeous spots along the way."

The discussion went back and forth, and eventually they decided to put it to a vote. The results were predictable. Seven for leaving Owen Bay and enjoying a leisurely cruise back down south and one for staying and searching for the gold.

After some more protesting and foot stomping, Molly gave in more or less graciously. Ian brought out the chart and

everyone pored over it, deciding on some great-looking anchorages on the route back to Vancouver.

Eventually, the younger crewmembers started yawning,
and Sophie declared bedtime for everyone. Soon the children
were settled in their bunks, leaving Captain Gunn alone in the
cockpit enjoying a last pipe.

LETICIA AWAKENED WITH a start. What was that noise?
Although she was an intrepid pirate and explorer, Leticia
had one fear that reduced her to a quivering wreck and that
was her fear of thunder and lightning. She reached across
the space between her bunk and Molly's and grabbed for her
sister's hand.

"Molly, wake up."

"Wassthematter," mumbled Molly from the depths of her
sleeping bag.

"I think it's thundering," squeaked Leticia.

Molly sat up, rubbed her eyes, and reached for her flashlight
from the shelf beside her bunk. She listened for a minute.

"That's not thunder," she said cautiously, "but I don't know
what it is."

"What's going on?" came a voice from amidships where
Sophie, Harriet, and Posy shared the large centre berth made
up from the settee in the saloon.

Molly and Leticia got out of their bunks and joined the three
other girls, now all awake and sitting up. Molly went aft and
shook Ian and Mark awake, and soon the entire crew was sitting together and listening to a very strange noise. It sounded

as if a waterfall had been created at the mouth of the bay and what they heard was water falling from a great height. But there was no waterfall anywhere near—or was there?

"I know what it is," said Ian suddenly. "It's the current flowing at maximum flood. Or ebb. Not sure which. I'd have to check the current tables, but I know it can run at as much as eight or nine knots in there, and when you add the whirlpools and overfalls the current creates, I think that's the noise you get. We're fine in here, no current at all."

Leticia heaved a sigh of relief, and they were all getting ready to head back to their bunks and go back to sleep when they heard something else. It sounded like footsteps heading along the dock from the shore towards their boat.

Everyone froze. There had been no sign of anyone else in Owen Bay, and they hadn't seen any other boats come into the bay since they arrived. The cabins all appeared deserted, so who could this be?

"I'm going to wake Uncle Bert," said Leticia. "I don't like this one bit. What if it's one of Brother XII's henchmen come to warn us off, or worse?"

She crept up the companionway ladder and tugged at her uncle's foot, which was poking out from the blankets covering him on his cockpit berth.

"Shhhhh..." she whispered as Captain Gunn sat bolt upright and opened his mouth in protest. "Can you hear that?"

"Hear what?" Captain Gunn replied quietly.

The cockpit had canvas sides that were lowered at night to provide Captain Gunn with the semblance of privacy from neighbouring boats. The crew had all crept up into the cockpit and sat quietly, listening hard.

The footsteps came closer and closer, and in the faint light of the moon glimmering through the canvas, the crew could see that everyone was frozen, listening intently, and gazing through the canvas on the side nearest to the dock. They could see nothing, but the footsteps kept coming until they stopped, apparently half a yard away from them on the dock.

All of a sudden Captain Gunn jumped up with a huge roar. "Who goes there?"

The entire crew gasped, then held their breaths and listened for an answer. None came. There was complete and utter silence—even the noise of the rapids was now just a murmur.

Captain Gunn leaned out of the opposite side of the cockpit and fumbled below where the dinghy was secured. He came up with an oar, peeled the dockside canvas back, and jumped (or rather scrambled, jumping being difficult for someone of his age and size) out onto the dock.

"Someone pass me a flashlight!" he yelled back at the crew.

Ian quickly reached through the gap in the canvas and handed him the large flashlight that was kept handy in the cockpit. They heard Captain Gunn set off up the dock and could see the glow of the flashlight fading away towards the ramp. A few minutes passed and then they heard him clomping back.

"What a rum thing," he said as he scrambled back on-board. "No sign of anyone, and they couldn't have got away so fast. We're tied up near the farthest end, and whoever it was couldn't

possibly have made it along the dock and up the ramp and disappeared without me seeing them."

"I thought this place felt peculiar," said Harriet. "I think it's
haunted."

"I don't know about haunted, but I think you're right," replied
Captain Gunn. "We'll check those current tables and get out
of here pronto in the morning. Now back to bed the lot of you.
There's no one there, and who knows. We may have just imagined those footsteps—creaking timbers on the dock, maybe."

Sophie had a hard time convincing Posy that they weren't
going to be boarded by pirates in the dead of night once she
fell asleep, but eventually everyone settled down and peace
returned to *South Islander*. However, Captain Gunn only dozed
for the rest of the night, and he did so with the oar kept handy
to bump any potential pirates on the head if they tried to board.

THE SUN WAS shining brightly before anyone woke up the next
morning. Harriet was the first to creep up on deck, and she sat
on the cabin top to enjoy the morning alone with her thoughts
before the others joined her and their usual cacophony dis-
turbed the quiet of a west coast morning.

And it was very, very quiet. At first Harriet couldn't figure
out what felt so strange, but after a few minutes she realized
that not only was the morning still and totally calm, with no
sound of rushing water from the rapids, but also there were no
birds chirping or any sound at all. No birds' wings swishing as
they flew overhead, no twittering from the trees on the shore,

nothing. As she sat there, a very peculiar feeling came over her. Something very odd was going on.

"Captain Gunn, please wake up," she said, panicking. What could be less ominous than a beautiful, cloudless morning? And yet, she felt that something dreadful was about to happen.

"What's up, Harriet?" asked Captain Gunn as he slowly rose from the horizontal to the perpendicular. "Did that ghost come back?"

"I don't know," she answered sheepishly, somewhat ashamed of her panic, "but something's not right."

The rest of the crew, awakened by the noise on deck, appeared in the cockpit. Leticia and Ian rolled up the canvas so that they could all see out, and Harriet joined them from her perch on the cabin roof.

All of a sudden, the boat started to rock, which was very odd given that they were tied to a solid dock and no one was moving around. Molly glanced at the shore and let out a screech.

"The trees are moving—look!" she sputtered.

Everyone looked towards the shore, and sure enough, the trees nearest the shoreline were swaying backwards and forwards, even though there wasn't a breath of wind. The dock appeared to be moving to and fro in waves, and the boat was squeaking and groaning in protest as her mooring lines were stretched and released by the motion of the dock.

"Quick!" yelled Captain Gunn. "I think we're having an earthquake. Cast off those lines as fast as you can. We'll stand off in the middle of the bay. Mark, fire up the engine as quick as you can. Just leave the lines on the dock."

In a matter of seconds, *South Islander* was drifting clear of land with her mooring lines hanging in the water off the edge of the dock. Mark had got the engine going, and they were soon idling in circles in the middle of the bay. The water was restless, and the whole bay seemed to be slopping around like the water in a bathtub when the occupants are playing and splashing. A deep rumbling that seemed to come from the very core of the earth broke the calm of the morning, and as they gazed in fascinated horror, the trees on the shore started snapping and toppling. A cabin that they could just see near the top of the dock seemed to dance and sway before disappearing with a crash into the bush. A large crack from the other side of the bay made them all swivel around in unison as a large lump of rock broke off an overhanging cliff and tumbled into the bay. It was as if a giant had picked up the bay and the land around it and was shaking it back and forth in fury.

Seconds spun out to seem like hours, but in fact it was only about four minutes later (Ian had glanced at his watch as they left the dock) when everything quietened down. There was silence in the cockpit, broken at last by Molly.

"We've survived an earthquake!" she exclaimed. "What a fantastic story we're going to have to tell when we get home."

Not everyone was quite as thrilled. Posy's face was white and she was clinging on to Sophie's hand. Leticia was doing her best to hold in her fear, telling herself that at least it hadn't been a thunderstorm, and the others were staring around the bay and wondering if it was all over.

"I think we'd better stay off the dock for a while. There could be aftershocks," said Captain Gunn. "Leticia, you go below and make us all a nice cup of tea. Best thing after a shock like this. Ian, I want you to take a careful look at the current tables and figure out the best time to get out of here. The sooner the better. I really don't much like this place."

"We're almost out of drinking water," said Sophie. "I wonder if there's a fresh stream where we can fill up the barrel."

"That place where we walked up to the lake had a good-looking stream, and I think I remember where there was a little waterfall close to the beach where we can fill the barrel," said Harriet. "We can put it into the dinghy and take it over there. If we sling it on an oar I'm pretty sure we can carry it, even when it's full of water."

For the next hour *South Islander* circled the bay while the crew sipped their mugs of tea, watching the shore for signs of more earthquakes. Everything settled down, and Captain Gunn deemed it safe to return to the dock. Soon they were once more tied up, and the whole party went up the dock to see the damage.

It was hard to imagine what the place had looked like before. Even though they had been derelict, at least the remaining cabins had been standing and might have been reinhabited with a little work. Now there was simply nothing left. The cabins were mostly just piles of rubble, good only for firewood. Great swathes of trees had fallen or were leaning up against the ones still upright. It had been a peculiar, spooky, uninhabited place before the earthquake; now it was completely devastated.

"The sooner we get out of here the better," said Captain Gunn. "Apart from everything else, I'm wondering how bad the damage is in Vancouver. Let's get that water barrel filled up and be on our way. What time did you say we could transit the rapids, Ian?"

"It's slack and turns to flood at half past two. If we leave then we can catch the first of the flood tide to help us along and all the way down to Surge Narrows. We'll have to wait a while before we can get through Beazley Passage and transit on the last of the flood when the current has quietened down. Once we get through there into Hoskyn Channel, there's not a lot of current to worry about."

Everyone was feeling a curious sense of loss and disappointment. Loss at the devastating change to the landscape, and disappointment that they had lost the trail of Brother XII. It was going to be hard to turn their backs on Owen Bay when it seemed probable that Brother XII had lived there, but they had simply run out of clues. It would take months to search every nook and cranny for the lost gold, and they didn't have months. At the most they could afford a few more days, and that would mean their cruise south would be a rushed affair. It had been an incredible adventure, but now their thoughts returned to the fact that they would be on a ship heading back to England before too long.

CHAPTER TEN

THE GOLDEN RAVEN

THE BARREL SAT amidships in the dinghy. Ian, Molly, Leticia, Harriet, and Sophie squeezed in around it and paddled up the bay to the spot by the stream where they had landed the day before. Mark was again fiddling with the engine, and Posy was ensconced in a corner of the saloon with her crayons and colouring book. Captain Gunn was studying the chart and planning their route back to Vancouver.

As the shore party approached the landing spot on the tiny beach, they saw that the earthquake had wreaked havoc here, as well as in the tiny settlement at the dock. Trees had fallen onto the beach, and when they clambered over them towards the stream they could see that the trail to the lake was completely blocked by fallen logs. The tumbledown buildings by the stream were now piles of splintered lumber. Harriet looked across to the tool shed they had observed the day before to see if it too had succumbed to the earthquake.

"Look at that bird!" she shouted, pointing towards the shed. "What's it got in its beak?"

The crew turned and looked at the large, shiny, jet-black raven sitting on top of what remained of the tool shed. Suddenly, it rose into the air with a tremendous flapping of wings, and just as it flew over their heads a shaft of sunlight caught the object in its beak. It was as if the bird was holding a miniature sun that gleamed and shimmered and threw off golden rays. In a second it was gone, flying low over the bay.

"What on earth was that?" wondered Molly. "I'm going over to take a look."

"Be careful you don't fall and twist your ankle getting over all those branches," warned her sister.

The rest of the crew watched as Molly clambered over logs and branches until she reached the pile of rubble that was once the tool shed. She started pulling pieces away and called to the others.

"Come on over, all of you. I see something, but we need all hands on deck to move this stuff."

The others followed in her path and were soon clearing a spot right in the middle of the remains of the shed. What Molly had seen was the glint of broken glass from under the wreckage, and when they pulled the last bit of rubble aside, they gave a collective gasp and then fell silent, gazing down into a hole.

Lined up under what had been the floor were several large Mason jars. Inside each one they could clearly see the glimmer of gold coins. One of the jars had fallen over and broken, and its contents were scattered on the ground. It was likely the raven had taken its coin from the broken jar.

The enormity of what they had found took a few minutes of stunned silence to sink in. Then Molly gave an enormous yell and started jumping up and down, nearly overbalancing and falling into the hole with the gold.

"We've found it, we've found it!" she shrieked. "Brother XII's gold, right here—and it would have stayed hidden forever if it wasn't for the earthquake!"

"How are we going to get it back to *South Islander?*" wondered Sophie. "It must weigh a ton."

"I think we should take one jar back to show Uncle Bert, and then maybe he can move the boat closer so we can ferry the dinghy back and forth," said Leticia.

"We're still going to need water," said Sophie. "We can't drink gold! Let's get that barrel filled up and then come back for one of the unbroken jars."

Somewhat reluctantly, the crew turned their backs on the gold and scrambled back over the fallen logs to the beach. The barrel had rings screwed into the metal bands that held it together, and they threaded a line through the rings and slung it on an oar. They carried it over to the stream, where they discovered that the waterfall they had noticed the day before had completely disappeared and the stream had changed course. Boulders had tumbled down and diverted the stream, but after a bit of exploration they found another spot where they could wedge the barrel under the lip of a slab of rock, over which the stream fell in a narrow torrent, just the right size to quickly fill the barrel through the open bung hole.

The full barrel was extremely heavy, and it took all of them to manhandle it back to the beach and safely stow it amidships in the dinghy. They left the dinghy floating with a line to a branch ashore and returned to the tool shed for the jar of gold. Between them, Molly and Ian were able to lift one of the jars out of the hole and struggled with it over the logs back to the dinghy. They pushed off from the shore and were soon alongside *South Islander*. Ian and Captain Gunn rigged up a pulley from the boom and the filled barrel was soon safely secured on its chocks on the foredeck. Meanwhile, Molly had been bursting in anticipation of showing the gold to her uncle, but managed to contain herself until the water was on-board and they were once again all sitting around the cockpit.

"I've got something to show you, Uncle Bert," she said mysteriously, and with that she pulled a coin out of her pocket and thrust it in his face. "There's ten jars full of these coins! We found them under an old shed that fell down in the earthquake. Look, there's one jar in the bottom of the dinghy. It's really heavy, so we'll have to go back for the rest. How much do you think it's all worth?"

Captain Gunn gazed at the coin in his hand and then leaned over the bulwarks and stared speechless at the glass jar lying in the bottom of the dinghy. It took him a few minutes to answer the question.

"I'm not sure what the current value of gold is, but at a very rough guess I'd say there's well over $100,000 worth with what you've got here and the other jars back in the shed."

For once, nobody knew what to say. Even Molly, intrepid pirate and terror of the seas, could not have imagined finding such a vast fortune.

"Brother XII really did turn all his ill-gotten gains into gold coins," she mused, once she found her voice again. "Gold never goes out of fashion, and he could have sold those coins off a few at a time to support him in his 'retirement.' The biggest mystery is where he ended up. There is no way he would put all that money under that shed and then never come back to get it. He must have come to a nasty end. Maybe he got dragged into the rapids and drowned."

"In any case, we can give this back to all his victims," said Harriet.

"First things first," said Captain Gunn. "I think the best plan is to move *South Islander* over and anchor as close as we can get to the gold. Then we'll load it on-board—I think we can store all those jars in the cockpit lockers, well padded with cushions. I want to catch that tide, so we must be motoring out of the bay by 2:30. It's a quarter to one now, so we'd better get moving."

It didn't take long to cast off from the dock, this time taking the mooring lines with them. Leticia and Harriet neatly coiled all the lines and stowed them in one of the aft lockers. The boat moved along the shoreline with Ian out on the bowsprit looking over into the clear waters of the bay. When they were about thirty yards away from the beach, he yelled back to Captain Gunn at the helm.

"I don't think we should go any farther in. Can I drop the anchor here?"

"Mark, put that engine into slow reverse," ordered Captain Gunn. "Ian, drop the anchor."

The anchor was dropped and the boat slowly reversed before coming to a full stop with the anchor line taut.

"All right, let's have a look at that gold of yours," said Captain Gunn.

He, Molly, Ian, and Leticia piled into the dinghy and rowed ashore. Captain Gunn had a bit of trouble heaving his bulk over the rough terrain and broken trees, but the remaining crew on the boat could see when he got there and was bending over the hole. They saw him stand upright, pulling a large spotted handkerchief out of his pocket. He stood wiping his forehead for a few minutes and then leaned down over the hole again. Then they saw Ian drop down into the hole and start passing up the jars. They were very heavy, and Molly and Leticia had to lean over the hole and grab each jar together, bringing them out of the hole and placing them in a gleaming, golden line on a flat log.

"I reckon each of those jars weighs well over thirty pounds," said Ian. "I think Captain Gunn underestimated the value of this lot. In any case, it's going to be a bit of a struggle getting them all back to the boat, and we need to hurry up to catch the tide." They were all sweating by the time they had transported the eight unbroken jars back to the beach. The coins from the broken jar were loaded into an empty basket, which was much easier to handle. Eventually all the gold was safely on the beach, and they took it in two loads back to *South Islander*, where Captain Gunn had rigged up a sling and a pulley off the boom.

"Don't want to drop any of this overboard," he said, "so be very, very careful loading it into the sling. Make sure it's centred and can't roll out."

There were a few scary moments when one of the jars shifted in the sling and looked likely to slide out and end up in the water. Captain Gunn managed to lean over the gunwales and steady it, and the crew soon had the rest of the jars of gold up on deck. Working two to a jar, they moved the treasure to its new hiding place under the cockpit cushions.

"Right," said Captain Gunn, as the last jar was stowed into its hiding place. "Let's get that anchor up and head out of here. We're just in time to get through those rapids at slack water. Oh, jolly good, Sophie, I was getting a bit peckish. Let's have those sandwiches as soon as we're under way."

Sophie and Leticia between them had made a pile of their new favourite sandwiches, peanut butter and marmalade, and as soon as *South Islander* was quietly chugging out of Owen Bay, the crew tucked into their lunch, having missed breakfast in all the excitement of earthquakes and treasure.

The Upper Rapids were calm as they passed through. It was hard to imagine that the dire warnings marked on the chart could ever turn this peaceful waterway into a churning, heaving, swirling torrent. They passed the entrance to Hole in the Wall and the small islands to starboard. Although none of them really believed in spirits or ghosts, they had all felt that the distinctly spooky atmosphere in Owen Bay. It was so different from their anchorage in the Octopus Islands, where they had felt nothing but the sheer beauty and peace of the place.

Once through the rapids, Ian took another look at the chart and checked his calculations. He figured that at the speed they were going they would need to kill some time on this side of the next set of rapids at Beazley Passage.

"Look here on the chart," he said. "There's a little bay on the Maurelle Island side of the channel, just past this small island. We can anchor in there for an hour or so and catch the last of the current through the pass. We don't want to go too soon—it says here that the current can run at as much as twelve knots."

The water was calm, and the scenery was spectacular. Everyone was feeling a bit dazed by the latest turn of events. Here they were, carrying a king's ransom in gold, having by sheer luck (with the unexpected help of an earthquake) unearthed the treasure that so many people had looked long and hard for. They hadn't found any trace of Brother XII, but what mattered was that all the innocent people he had cheated were going to get their money back.

They found the nook that Ian had noted on the chart, nosed in, and anchored fairly close to shore. There was a strip of beach and a small clearing, and in the clearing they could see a small cabin, which seemed to have survived the earthquake intact.

"I don't want anyone going ashore," said Captain Gunn. "I think it's unlikely our villains are still on the island—they probably hitched a lift off some poor unsuspecting boater—but I don't want to take any risks. So just sit tight, and we'll be on our way through the pass in an hour or so."

The words were barely out of his mouth when they heard yelling from the shore. The crew turned towards land and saw the five unkempt sailors from the Black Pearl emerge from the cabin, shouting and waving their arms.

"Not rescued after all," said Molly wryly. "Well, they can think again if they are hoping for us to pick them up. As far as I'm concerned they can stay here forever."

Before anyone could stop her, Molly jumped out of the cockpit, ran along the side deck, and, cupping her hands around her mouth, shouted at the top of her voice towards the shore.

"We hope you rot here forever! Don't worry, though. We're going to call the police and they can come and pick you up. Hope you can live on seaweed for a few more days!"

"Molly, Molly, get down!" shrieked her sister.

"Don't be foolish!" yelled Captain Gunn. "You're just baiting them. We know they have a gun!"

The others joined in, pleading with Molly to get off the deck and back into the relative safety of the cockpit, but their warnings came too late. There was a loud bang, quickly followed by another. That split second seemed to expand into a long, silent minute, and then Molly gave a strangled cry from the foredeck.

"I've been shot!" she declared, her voice a mixture of shock and awe.

Sophie was the first to react. She bolted down below and grabbed her as-yet-unused first-aid kit, arriving back in the cockpit at the same time as Molly, who had scrambled astern, clutching her left arm with her right.

Sophie grabbed a wad of cotton wool and some gauze out of the first-aid kit and applied pressure to Molly's arm.

"It's all right," she said to Molly, though she was far from sure it was. The main thing was for the person in charge of first aid to keep calm. She'd assembled the kit with thoughts of scraped knees and headaches, not gunshot wounds. Sophie had been thrown into the deep end as the designated nurse on-board, but she caught her lip between her teeth and bent to her task with determination.

Everyone's faces were white with shock, except Molly's, which was grey, and Captain Gunn's, which was bright red with fury.

"Keep your heads down, everyone!" bellowed Captain Gunn, disobeying his own order by standing up and yelling: "How dare you shoot at a boat full of children! You're going to jail for a very long time if I have anything to say about it!"

The reply came in the form of two more shots, one of which clipped the mainmast and sent a shower of splinters down on the cockpit.

"We're going to have to get out of here pronto," said Captain Gunn. "Your mothers are never going to forgive me for taking you in range of a bunch of madmen. Ian and Leticia, I hate to do this, but I don't see any other way. Can you wriggle snakelike along the side deck farthest from shore and get that anchor up? We'll get the engine going and drive forwards over the anchor so it should come up fairly easily. Everyone else, I want you below."

"I think the bullet went right through the fleshy part of her arm," said Sophie, looking up from her patient. "There's lots of blood, but there are two wounds, one on either side, and I can't feel the bullet."

Molly had now turned from grey to a greenish shade of pale and was sitting in a corner of the cockpit looking as though she might be sick at any moment. Sophie put her arm around her and steered her down the companionway, where Harriet, Posy, Mark, and Leticia had already gone.

Mark had been getting ready to start the engine, and on Captain Gunn's command he pushed the starter and put the engine in gear. The boat crept forwards, still tethered to its anchor, and Captain Gunn steered so that the starboard side was away from shore.

"All right, you two. Wriggle along on the starboard side deck, and when you get to the foredeck keep your heads down. We didn't put down much anchor line for such a short stay, but it's going to be a bit tricky getting the anchor up from a lying position. Put your backs into it and pull as fast as you can."

Ian and Leticia quickly wriggled on their stomachs to the foredeck, and were soon hauling up the anchor as if their lives depended on it—which, to be fair, they did.

The final bit of chain rattled up with the anchor attached, and Captain Gunn ordered the engine full speed ahead, steering the boat as quickly as possible away from the shore. It appeared that either the crew on-shore had run out of ammunition or they realized it was pointless to fire off any more shots. The last thing the *South Islander* crew saw as they sailed away was the five men jumping up and down, yelling, and shaking their fists. *South Islander* had escaped, but one of its crew was in grave danger.

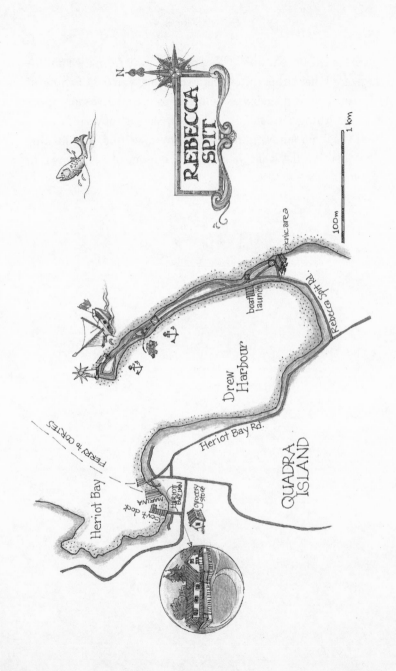

CHAPTER ELEVEN
A WOUNDED CREWMEMBER

C APTAIN GUNN steered *South Islander* out of the cove and turned to port, heading for the passage through Surge Narrows, marked on the chart as Beazley Passage. The narrows were a maze of small islands and other channels, but the crew had studied the chart earlier and it was clear that the only safe way through was Beazley Passage.

"We are far too early to be safely transiting this," muttered Captain Gunn.

They had all been in some sticky situations before, but this was the first time anyone had been seriously injured and Captain Gunn looked extremely worried and distracted. He kept glancing below, where Sophie was administering first aid to Molly, and then back to the chart and tide tables that were open on one of the cockpit seats.

"We need to get Molly to a doctor pronto, and I don't want to hang around this side of the narrows with those madmen letting off potshots in our direction. We'll just have to take our chances going through with a pretty big current. We should be all right, but I'm a bit nervous about those whirlpools that show on the chart. As long as we don't lose power and have steerage, I think we'll make it. Mark, stand by at the engine controls and be ready to do as I say, when I say so."

Mark was in the companionway with one eye on Captain Gunn and the other on the engine controls, ready to obey orders as soon as they were issued.

Meanwhile, Sophie had her first-aid kit spread open on the table in the saloon and was busy ministering to the injured Molly, who was sitting on the settee propped up on cushions with her arm in the process of being bandaged. She seemed to have recovered somewhat from the initial shock and was looking quite pleased with herself.

"Imagine—shot at by real pirates after we've scooped the gold from under their noses! We've never had an adventure like this before. Definitely worth getting shot at!"

"That's the shock talking," said Sophie as she neatly tied the ends of the bandage and rested Molly's arm on a pillow. "I'm going to make you a nice cup of sweet tea— that's the best thing for shock. And you need to stay quite still and rest. I've only done basic first aid and made sure the bleeding has stopped. You need to get to a doctor as soon as possible."

The rest of the crew were now in the cockpit with Captain Gunn, watching as the boat headed for the narrow passage. As they got closer, they could see the current swirling against the rocks and the ominous whirlpools in the narrowest part of the channel.

"It's going to be quite unsteady going through here. Those currents and whirlpools can grab a boat and swing it around. Amazing power in that water when it's going at maximum flow. Ian, I want you to stand by to give me a hand with the wheel if I need it. You others, grab a stanchion and stay seated."

The boat was now flying along and being sucked into the passage. There was no way on earth they could have turned and headed back to wait for slacker water. Captain Gunn was gripping the wheel and chewing his lip as he steered the boat towards the gap. They could clearly see calm water on the other side, but in the pass it was churning and eddying, and the boat was being pushed one way and then the other. Suddenly they skimmed the edge of a whirlpool, and the mast seemed to dip to starboard as the bow tried to turn towards the rocks on one side of the channel. Captain Gunn yelled for Ian to help him, and between them they wrestled with the wheel to turn the boat back to port. The boat straightened up, and all at once it was as if they had been spit out of the mouth of a fast-flowing river into the calm waters of a bay. They were through!

TWENTY MINUTES LATER they were secured to the dock at the Surge Narrows store on Read Island. Captain Gunn had barely waited for the boat to come alongside before leaping off it and running as fast as he could up the ramp and into the store, leaving the others to secure all the lines and tidy up. Sophie stayed below with Molly, who was resting on the settee—something she would never have considered doing under any other circumstances than having been shot in the arm.

"Quick! I need to radio for a doctor," panted Captain Gunn as he flung himself through the door of the store. It looked as if the building had taken a tremendous shaking from the earthquake. The shelves that lined the wall behind the counter were almost empty, as most of their former contents were scattered all over the floor.

"Calm down, old chap," replied the store owner from behind the counter, where he was clearing up the mess. After a moment he rose up leisurely to greet his visitor. "What seems to be the problem?"

Trying not to garble, Captain Gunn gave the short version of the story, finishing up with a plea to get onto the radio as soon as possible, if not sooner, and summon a doctor to tend to Molly.

The store owner looked pensive for a full fifteen seconds, causing a bulging vein in Captain Gunn's right temple to nearly burst. Finally he spoke. "Well, let me see now. I think the best thing to do would be to call up Jim Spilsbury on the radio and see if he can pick up your niece in his float plane and take her to the hospital in Powell River."

"Yes, yes, that's a great idea," gasped Captain Gunn, bending over and doing his best to get his breath back. (Running was not part of his daily routine.)

But instead of rushing off to make the call, the store owner kept talking. "Now, there is a nurse and first-aid station on Quadra Island, but in the case of a gunshot wound I suppose she would probably want your niece to go the hospital anyway, so we can likely save some time by getting her there directly with Jim."

"Please, please call now!" yelled Captain Gunn, jumping up and down in desperation.

The store owner blinked at Captain Gunn. His expression—or maybe it was the fact that he was the slowest individual on the planet—made him look rather like a turtle. Finally, he turned and went into a back room. After what seemed like hours but was in fact minutes, Captain Gunn could hear him talking over the two-way radio. The conversation was mercifully short—thank goodness Jim Spilsbury sensed the urgency of the situation—and the store owner returned.

"I was lucky—Jim was at his place on Savary Island, and he has his float plane pulled up on the beach. He's going straight out there and should be here in less than an hour. Here, sit down. You look as if you're about to keel over."

Captain Gunn had gone a paler shade of grey and slumped into a chair beside the counter.

"My sister would never, ever forgive me if anything happened to any of those children. What am I saying—something *has* happened to one of them. She'll have my guts for garters. I knew those fellows were dangerous—we should have stayed well away instead of provoking them."

He was near tears and mopping his brow with a large red-spotted handkerchief. The store owner went into the back again and returned with a large tot of something amber in a shot glass.

"Here, my good man. I think you need this. Medicinal brandy. Take it in one swig and you'll soon feel better."

Captain Gunn downed the contents of the glass, choked and gasped a few times, and then sat up straight and pulled himself together.

"We'll need to contact the police as well," he said. "Not only are those villains still on Maurelle Island taking potshots at passing boaters, but I need to tell them about the gold. If anyone finds out what we've got aboard, we'll be a sitting target for any Tom, Dick, or Harry robber who has access to a boat."

The store owner disappeared once more, and this time the conversation over the radio went on for quite some time. Eventually he returned.

"It would take the police quite some time to get a boat and make it all the way up here. I've had a good long chat with a Mountie, and we've decided the best thing to do is for you to head back down to Lund and they will meet you there. With any luck the hospital will have patched up your niece and Jim can fly her back from Powell River to meet you and the rest of your crew in Lund. We think it's pretty safe for you to sail from here to Lund without being bothered. Don't forget, no one knows that you have the gold on-board except me, and I can swear on my mother's grave that I won't be telling anyone until it's all out in the open. I think you can count on a fair bit of publicity once the gold is safely in the hands of the police and the story leaks out."

Captain Gunn sighed in relief. Turtle-like or not, the store owner was calm and level-headed. He thanked him profusely and hurried back down to the boat.

"Sophie, I want you to go with Molly to the hospital. Can you pack a few things for the two of you? Then we'll get Molly on deck and wait for Jim Spilsbury's float plane. Should be here very soon."

Sophie quickly sorted out a few things for her and Molly and packed them neatly into one of the rucksacks. Molly was helped up on deck and seated in the cockpit, propped up on pillows. Meanwhile, Leticia had slipped below and made a huge pot of tea—that great British cure-all for any traumatic situation.

The entire crew assembled in the cockpit and for a moment there was dead silence. The shock of the day's adventures had sunk in. They could hardly believe they had been shot at, spun through the rapids, and all come out the other side more or less in one piece. And to cap it all off, they were in possession of a fortune in gold coins.

"What's going to happen to the gold?" asked Mark.

"The Mounties are going to meet us in Lund and take charge of it. I believe they are bringing an armed guard from Vancouver to accompany it back there, where I imagine it will be valued and put in a bank vault. The lawyers will have to figure out who gets what, and that could all take some time. I'm pretty sure, though, that there will be a substantial reward for finding it," said Captain Gunn as he scanned the horizon. "For now we just need to make sure that Molly is taken care of—and look! I think I see the plane coming."

The crew could see the plane approaching. Flying low up Hoskyn Channel between Quadra and Read Islands, it turned in towards the dock, swooped down, and landed not far from shore, sending up wings of spray from its two floats. It settled down in the water like a bird coming in to land and then taxied over to the dock. As it came close, the engine stopped, the door opened, and Jim Spilsbury stepped out on the float with a mooring line. He had obviously done this before. He brought the plane neatly in and stepped out onto the dock, cleating the line and bringing the plane to a dead stop.

"Hello there," he said. "I hear you've had a spot of bother and have a casualty that needs a lift to the hospital."

"I'm jolly glad to see you," said Captain Gunn. "Molly is our patient, and I'm hoping you can take Nurse Sophie with you too."

"No problem—plenty of room," he replied. "Let's get them aboard and we'll be off. I've radioed the hospital in Powell River to expect us, and they're sending an ambulance down to the dock to meet us."

Molly was helped off the boat and up into the plane. This was a bit of a manoeuvre since she had only one good arm, but with Sophie ahead and Jim behind they were able to get her settled in the back seat. Sophie sat next to Jim, who quickly started the engine again.

"I'll leave a message for you at the hotel in Lund," he yelled over the noise of the engine. "I'll get your niece and her friend back to you there as soon as she's been patched up and they've released her from the hospital. Don't worry, she'll be in good hands. I know most of the doctors there, and they're a fine bunch. She'll be good as new in a couple of days."

Ian cast off the mooring line, and the plane moved away from the dock and into the channel. With the engine revved to maximum, it ploughed through the water until it gained enough speed to heave its floats out of the water and start skimming across the channel. Soon the line of wake shortened and then disappeared as the plane lifted off and headed south until it could no longer be seen.

SOUTH ISLANDER FOLLOWED the same course as the plane, but at a fraction of its speed. It was getting late in the afternoon, and after careful consultation with the chart they decided to go as far as Heriot Bay, tie up for the night, and then make it back to Lund the next day. Everyone was subdued by the events of the day and the thought of Molly and Sophie arriving at the hospital and what the doctors would be doing to their wounded crewmember.

As dusk was falling they cleared the light on the end of Rebecca Spit and headed over to the dock in front of the old hotel.

"We'll have a bite to eat in the pub and then it's early to bed for all of you," said Captain Gunn. "I won't be happy until I've heard what's happened to Molly, so we'll make an early start tomorrow and we should be in Lund by early afternoon. Leticia, I believe there's a general store here, so you can stock up on a few things if you need to."

Heriot Bay had suffered very little earthquake damage compared with Owen Bay, which had apparently born the brunt of it. People were lounging on the veranda in front of the hotel, talking about the quake. Although the experience had been a bit of a shock for everyone, the worst they had suffered was a few broken windows and pictures that had fallen off the wall.

That evening the crew had their first taste of a genuine Canadian hamburger, served with glasses of Coca Cola for the children and a large mug of draft beer for Captain Gunn.

"These are delicious," said Mark through a large mouthful. "I don't know why we don't have them in England. Maybe we can make our fortune by selling hamburgers back home."

"I think we've already made our fortune," laughed Leticia. "I'll take bags of gold over hamburgers any day."

"Shush," said Ian. "Remember it's all still on the boat. We don't want anyone hearing us talk about gold."

The crew looked around, but no one seemed to be taking much notice of them and they quickly finished their meal and headed back to the boat. Leticia made a detour to the store and got some fresh milk and a large loaf of bread that would see them through until they got back to Lund.

Once they were all tucked up in their bunks, everyone could feel the absence of Molly and Sophie. Posy was not happy about being without her big sister, but Harriet did her best, and eventually quiet descended on the boat. Captain Gunn sat on deck with his pipe for quite some time before bunking down. It had been a long and stressful day.

What will tomorrow bring? he thought to himself.

WHAT TOMORROW BROUGHT was fog. Thick, thick fog that obscured the old inn at the top of the ramp and was so dense that they couldn't even see the foredeck from the cockpit.

"I just don't want to wait out this fog," said Captain Gunn. "We need to get to Lund and find out how Molly is doing. Ian, bring out all the charts and tide tables and let's plot a course. It'll be good practice for you, and if we do our sums right we won't have any problems. The biggest thing is that we don't want to get run down in the fog. Mark, do you know where that portable foghorn is stowed?"

Captain Gunn and Ian spread the charts out on the cockpit table. With a pencil, parallel ruler, and dividers they plotted their course. They would need to cross Sutil Channel towards Cortes Island, negotiate Uganda Passage (taking account of the currents), sail down the western side of Cortes (avoiding the myriad rocks that dotted the shore), round the southernmost tip of the island, and then set a course for Lund. Soon the chart was criss-crossed with pencil lines and notations giving the correct compass bearings.

"We'll cast off in an hour to catch the best current through Uganda Passage," said Captain Gunn.

Leticia, not wanting to be compared unfavourably with the chief cook, prepared a mammoth breakfast. Bacon, fried tomatoes, scrambled eggs, thick hunks of bread with lots of butter and marmalade, and a huge pot of tea were all set out inside the saloon. Outside the air was cold and clammy with the fog shrouding the boat, but inside Captain Gunn had lit the wood stove, and it was warm and cozy and smelled deliciously of bacon.

"What a stupendous breakfast," said Mark, "almost as good as Sophie makes."

His comment was met with laughs and reassurances to Leticia that her breakfast was equal to anything Sophie could have produced.

After breakfast, Ian, Leticia, and Captain Gunn went on deck to ready the boat, Mark stood by the engine controls, and Harriet and Posy did the washing up. Soon the boat was chugging away from the dock with the two captains setting a compass course out of the harbour and across the channel towards Cortes Island.

FOUR HOURS LATER they were approaching Lund. At least, that was what they thought, as the fog was still so thick they could barely see the bowsprit. Mark had spent the voyage alternating between checking the engine and blasting off the portable foghorn at regular intervals. So far they hadn't been run down by any of the vessels that plied these waters in the summertime. Probably any sensible recreational boater was tied up or anchored and enjoying a day below decks. However, there were still the tugs and other commercial boats that they had seen plenty of during their trip, so Mark was playing a very important role in keeping them safe.

"Put that engine into slow," called Captain Gunn to Mark, who was hovering in the companionway. "I'm pretty sure we should be seeing the end of the dock anytime in the next five minutes."

They did. Leticia had been posted on the foredeck as lookout, and suddenly she gave a Molly-like whoop.

"The dock is dead ahead!" she yelled back to the cockpit. "Steer a bit to port and you'll clear the end and make it inside the breakwater."

Five minutes later they had found a spot on the dock and were securely moored. The whole crew headed up the ramp towards the hotel, where Captain Gunn hoped to contact Jim Spilsbury for an update on Molly's condition.

The hotel had sustained some damage in the earthquake. A couple of windows had broken and were boarded up, and one corner of the veranda had fallen down. But the historic hotel was still standing and open for business.

As they entered the hotel lobby two girls, one with her arm in a sling, rose from the sofa, and the rest of the crew ran forwards with cries of:

"Molly, you're back!"

"How's your arm?"

"How did you get back here so quickly?"

"What was it like flying in the float plane?"

"They didn't even keep me overnight," said Molly with a grin. "It was just a flesh wound, and they cleaned it up and re-bandaged it, but really they said that Sophie had done as good a job as they could! Jim flew us back here yesterday evening, and the hotel gave us a room for the night. The flying

was incredible! I'm going to get my pilot's licence when I get
back home!"

Captain Gunn was sitting down mopping his brow.

"Thank goodness," he said. "I wasn't looking forward to telling your mother I'd had to leave you behind in the hospital."

"Oh, don't be such a baby, Uncle Bert," laughed Molly. "I'm
fine, and Mother will be thrilled to hear the story."

"I'm not so sure about that," replied her uncle, "but all's well
that ends well, and now we just need to worry about getting rid
of this gold."

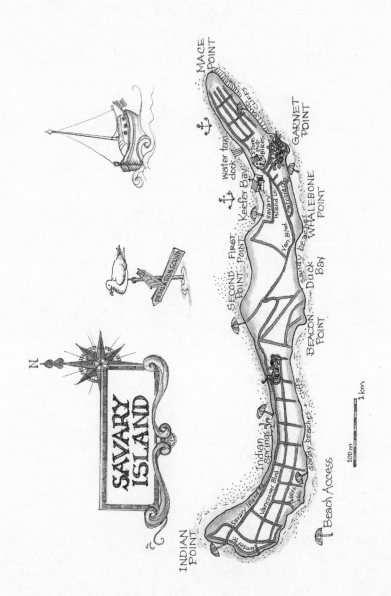

SAVARY ISLAND

N

INDIAN POINT

MACE POINT

GARNET POINT

WHALEBONE POINT

BEACON POINT

Duck Bay

sandy beaches

Van. Blvd.

Savary Island Rd.

First Point

Second Point

Keefer Bay

water taxi dock

DISRUPTION SOUND

Indian Springs

sandy beaches + cliffs

Savary Island Blvd.

Vancouver Blvd.

Sunset Dr.

Beach Access

100 m   1 km

CHAPTER TWELVE

SUNNY, SANDY SAVARY ISLAND

THE THREE CAPTAINS, two mates, two able seamen (Harriet thought she should be promoted to second mate), and one ship's baby (Posy was still rebelling against this title) all sat around a table in the hotel's coffee shop drinking hot chocolate and eating enormous cinnamon buns from the local bakery.

"Oh, look, here comes Jim, and it looks like he's brought a Mountie with him," said Molly through a mouthful of bun.

Their old friend Jim was accompanied by a younger man, who was not dressed in the scarlet uniform they had expected of a Mountie but in a uniform with shoulder patches that clearly identified him as a member of that famous police force.

"This is Sergeant Struthers from Powell River," said Jim. "He's brought an armoured truck and guard and is going to get that gold back to Vancouver and into the hands of the proper authorities."

Jim introduced each member of the crew to the sergeant, and then the two of them sat down and ordered coffee and their own cinnamon buns.

"Looks like you lot have succeeded where everyone else failed," said the sergeant, who had told them to call him Pete. "There've been many treasure seekers over the past few years, but none came up with so much as a brass farthing."

"Well, we wouldn't have found it at all if it hadn't been for the earthquake," said Ian. "Was there any damage in Vancouver?"

"There were a fair few broken windows, and some brickwork came down, but apart from that we were lucky. Seems that you might have had it stronger up here. I noticed a few cracks in the pavement outside the hotel, as well as those broken windows. But in any case, we dodged a bullet. They've been predicting the Big One for years—this was just a reminder that it could happen any day," said Pete. "Now, about the gold. Tell me roughly how much you found and I can give you a very rough guess at its worth."

"There were nine unbroken quart jars and one broken one with most of the coins lying nearby. I reckon the ravens got a few, so there'll be some gold-plated nests nearby!" said Captain Gunn. "I've done a rough calculation and I think each jar weighs about thirty pounds—it was quite a job getting them all on-board."

Pete was scribbling on a piece of paper. "That's around 4,800 ounces, and the current value of gold is around $35 per ounce."

Captain Gunn was right there with his own scrap of paper. "Yes, that's what I figured but I wasn't sure what it was worth per ounce."

The sergeant and the captain were racing neck and neck to do the arithmetic, and both put down their pencils and grinned at the same time.

"The whole lot is worth about $170,000," said Pete as Captain Gunn nodded in agreement. "I believe there is a substantial reward being offered by the lawyer who is representing all those defrauded by Brother xii. Not sure exactly what it will be, but I'm pretty sure you'll be going home richer than you were when you arrived."

The crew sat in silence. Then Harriet voiced what everyone was thinking.

"We didn't do it for the reward. We just wanted to find the treasure so people like Joe could get their money back and get on with their lives. Brother xii was a truly evil person, and we're glad he's probably dead and that the loot will go back to its rightful owners."

"Nonetheless, you will get a reward, and I think you should all take your share and do something worthy with it. Those people wouldn't have seen a penny of their lost fortunes if it wasn't for you lot," replied Pete.

Putting the matter of rewards to one side, and after finishing their refreshments, the whole gang headed down to the dock. At the top of the ramp they were joined by a big, beefy security guard carrying a rifle and with a revolver and truncheon on his belt. The gold was going to be in good hands.

After several trips with a large wheelbarrow, the gold was safely in the back of the armoured truck, which had been backed up to the top of the dock. A small crowd gathered but was kept at a distance by the guard. Once everything was loaded, Pete got Captain Gunn to sign a receipt.

The crew invited Sergeant Pete aboard for a quick tour of *South Islander* before leaving for Vancouver. Captain Gunn got his home phone number in Vancouver in case he had any technical questions about the life of a Mountie to add to his book.

"It's almost done, but it will make a nice last chapter if I can add a bit about how a Mountie does his job nowadays," said Captain Gunn.

As Pete was stepping ashore, Molly remembered she had a question.

"What's going to happen to those villains? Are they still stranded on Maurelle Island?" she asked.

"We sent a boat out from Campbell River to pick them up. Apparently they were only too happy to be taken into custody. Playing Robinson Crusoe had lost its appeal! They're in a heap of trouble because apparently that boat they wrecked was stolen, but of course, the most serious offence is shooting you! Fortunately, they'd only been in custody five minutes when most of the crew starting singing like canaries and pointing the finger at their 'captain.' The other four agreed that he was the one with the gun—they never laid a finger on it. I think that il *capitano* will be charged with attempted murder, and the others will get a deal for testifying against him. That means it's very unlikely that any of you will have to come back for a trial."

"That's a shame," replied Molly. "I'd have been very happy to come back to Vancouver and point a finger at him in court. What a story that would make!"

Reluctantly, Pete took his leave of *South Islander* and her crew and climbed into the armoured truck beside the guard. With many waves and promises of meeting up in Vancouver, the truck set off on the long trip back down south.

After a day swathed in fog, the sun was at last burning through and shining dimly over the village. After dinner, the crew sat round the cockpit reliving their adventures. It seemed they were coming to the end of it all, but they still had to get the boat back to Vancouver and had several days spare for the trip.

"Well, we've done what we set out to do—found the treasure! I say we look at the last few days as a holiday, pure and simple," said Captain Gunn. "What would you like to do tomorrow? We can take our time heading back down the coast—how about a day on the beach over on Savary Island?"

As soon as the words "Savary Island" were out of his mouth, they were hailed by Jim from the dock. He joined them in the cockpit to tell them all about Savary and its splendid beaches.

"I'm heading back over to my cottage right now—couldn't go anywhere until now because of the fog," he said. "Why don't you stop by for tea tomorrow after you've had enough of being cooked on the beach?"

Everyone agreed this was a splendid idea and watched as Jim hopped back into his float plane, taxied out from the dock, and took off towards Savary.

THE NEXT DAY dawned bright and sunny and promised to be very hot—a perfect day for playing on the beach.

Right after breakfast, they cast off, and the boat pulled out of the harbour and headed the short distance over to Savary Island. The island was a long sliver of sand and trees with a dock on the north side. They approached the shore cautiously, with the boat moving at idle speed.

"We need to be careful that we don't go too far in towards the beach. It's shallow quite a way out, and the tide is dropping. We don't want to end up aground and lying on our side," said Captain Gunn.

With some careful studying of the chart and a few throws of the lead line by Ian to establish the approximate depth of the water, they picked a spot, dropped the anchor, and paddled ashore in two loads.

The water close to the beach was deliciously warm, and the sand was hot on their feet as the whole party stood shading their eyes and deciding where to go. An exceedingly plump old lady sitting in a deck chair shaded by an umbrella noticed their indecision.

"The beach on the other side of the island is even better," she said as she sipped from a tall glass of lemonade and nibbled on a plate of sandwiches. "Just walk up the road to the top and then take the next turning on the left. You'll find a path to the beach on the south side of the island. People say there isn't a better beach closer than the Caribbean, but I think they're wrong. In my opinion you won't find a better beach anywhere in the world."

Leaving the woman to her sedentary afternoon, they all headed up the sandy road, passing a row of cottages that fronted the beach they had landed on. There were children riding bicycles up and down the road and people sitting out in front of their cottages, while others paddled and swam. There was even a tennis court along the road where a game of mixed doubles was in progress. The whole place had the feeling of a wonderful summer resort where time stood still and memories that would last a lifetime were created every minute of every day.

"I think that one must be Jim's," said Captain Gunn, pointing to a neat cottage just before the road headed up the hill. "We'll stop in there on our way back."

Captain Gunn was puffing and mopping his face with his handkerchief when they got to the top of the hill, but the walk was pleasantly shaded until they arrived at the head of the beach trail, when they were again in the full glare of the sun. The view from the top was magnificent—the calm, blue sea stretched away from the miles of sandy beach, and a view of Vancouver Island was visible in the distance. They slithered down the steep trail to the beach and ran to dip their toes in the water.

"It's even warmer than the other side," said Posy, splashing happily. "Can I practise my swimming, Sophie?"

"Yes, let's all get into our bathers and go for a swim," said Sophie. "Look over there—a perfect changing room."

Dotting the beach were a number of shelters made from driftwood, apparently made to provide shade from the blazing sun. They hung a towel across the entrance of the nearest one, and it became a perfect spot to get into their bathing suits. Once everyone had changed, Captain Gunn commandeered the shelter and announced he was going to nap for the next couple of hours.

"Our adventures have worn me out," he said. "I need a rest from the lot of you, so try not to find any more treasure or enrage another bunch of villains." And so saying, he manoeuvred his large bulk inside the shelter, made a pillow from a spare towel, and was soon snoring away.

Because of her sling, Molly was only able to wade in up to her knees, but the others splashed about and practised their swimming strokes. Ian worked on his crawl, doing lengths parallel to the beach. Harriet and Sophie coached Posy, who had just learned to swim that spring, and Mark and Leticia had fun doing flying leaps into the water. It was shallow a long way out, which accounted for the incredible warmth of the water. Eventually they had had enough and returned to Captain Gunn, who wasn't too happy to be woken up.

"There was a place to buy ice cream at the top of the hill," cajoled Molly. As the injured one in the party, she felt she had a right to demand special treats.

"All right, all right," grumbled her uncle. "I suppose getting myself up that path is a small price to pay for the fact I'm not sitting in a hospital waiting room trying to figure out how to tell your mother that you've been seriously injured. Let's go, then we'll drop in on Jim before heading back over to Lund. This isn't a good place to anchor for more than a couple of hours, especially if it starts to blow. We'll spend the night in Lund and then make an early start tomorrow."

After helping Captain Gunn up the path, two pushing him from behind and two pulling him from in front, they were soon sitting in the shade outside the tiny store and licking enormous ice cream cones. Everything in Canada seemed to be bigger than at home. Hamburgers, ice cream cones, villains, scenery, treasure—everything was larger, more extreme, more villainous, more magnificent. It was going to be hard to describe their experiences when they got home, and probably everyone who heard their stories would think they were exaggerating.

Jim was sitting on his deck enjoying a glass of beer when they all trooped up his garden path. A few minutes later, Captain Gunn was sipping his own ice-cold beer while the children had a bottle of Coca Cola each. This was a drink unknown to them before they came to Canada, and it had quickly replaced lemonade as their favourite summer beverage.

They didn't stay long. Back on *South Islander*, they headed over to Lund for their last night before starting the long trek back to Vancouver.

IT WAS WELL past midnight by the luminous dial on Ian's watch when Captain Gunn came below to tell them to wake up and come on deck. Sophie wasn't too keen on waking Posy, but orders were orders. She wrapped her little sister in a blanket and joined the others on deck.

"What is it?" asked Harriet, gasping in awe.

The whole sky was lit by an eerie green glow as curtains of light shimmered across the sky. It was as if a ghostly theatre performance was about to start with the actors behind the curtains ready to make their appearance as soon as the curtains parted. Perhaps a phantom stage manager had opened the back door of the theatre and a wind was blowing the curtains so that they appeared as rippling waves of light.

"It's called the Northern Lights," said Captain Gunn. "It's very unusual to see them this far south—normally you get them much farther north. Take a good long look, because you're unlikely to ever see them again, unless you take up Arctic exploration."

"Yes, but what causes it?" Harriet wanted to know.

"I believe it's caused by collisions between electrically charged particles from the sun that enter the earth's atmosphere," replied Captain Gunn, "but you can look it up in the encyclopaedia when you get home."

The crew sat for over an hour watching the incredible display before Sophie insisted they all go back to bed. With all their worries about Molly put to rest, the treasure in safe hands, and another few days of cruising to look forward to, they were asleep before Captain Gunn had settled his large bulk into a comfortable position in the cockpit and started his nightly serenade of gentle snores.

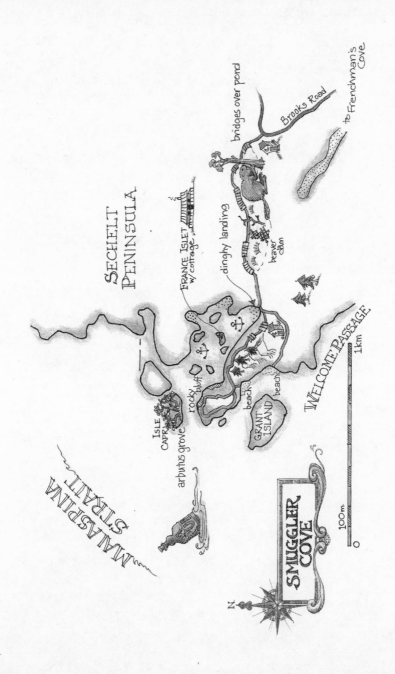

SECHELT PENINSULA

MALASPINA STRAIT

bridges over pond

Brooks Road

to Frenchman's Cove

FRANCE ISLET
w/ cottage

dinghy landing

beaver dam

Isle
Capri

arbutus grove

rocky bluff

beach

beach

GRANT
ISLAND

WELCOME PASSAGE

SMUGGLER
COVE

N

0   100m

1km

CHAPTER THIRTEEN
VANCOUVER AGAIN

B Y NOON THE NEXT DAY Savary Island was fading astern and they were motoring south between Texada Island and the Sunshine Coast. It was hot—very, very hot—and most of the crewmembers were already regretting their long play on the beach the day before. Sophie was busy with her first-aid kit, dabbing calamine lotion on burnt shoulders and noses, and today she was very strict about covering up and wearing hats.

"I'm boiling," complained Posy, who was sitting in the shade of the awning Captain Gunn had rigged over the cockpit. "Can't we stop and go swimming?"

"Nowhere good to stop along here," replied Captain Gunn. "How about hauling up some buckets of nice cold seawater and dousing yourselves?"

Soon everyone was up on the foredeck taking turns with the bucket. Ian had attached a long line to the handle and soon had the knack of swinging it in such a way as to bring it up almost full.

"It's not fair," wailed Molly. "I can't get my arm wet."

The rest of them were soaked within minutes, but relieved to be much cooler, and sat on towels in the cockpit enjoying the view of the sparkling water, scenic coastline, and mountains of Vancouver Island in the distance.

All of a sudden Leticia, who had stayed up on the foredeck, cried out.

"I think it's a whale!" she shouted back to the rest of the crew.

Sure enough, about a hundred yards off the bow, they saw the dorsal fin and a glimpse of a large tail, before the animal disappeared below the water.

"That's odd," said Harriet, observant as always. "We're in almost the exact same spot that we saw the porpoises on the way up."

Everyone's eyes were glued to the spot where the whale had appeared and then disappeared, and after about five minutes they were rewarded by the sight of not one, but three dorsal fins, heading in the same direction as they were. One whale's nose appeared, followed by the rest of its body so that it appeared to be standing up out of the water. It seemed to hover for a few seconds before plunging back into the water with a tremendous splash. After that the fins appeared a few more times at ever increasing distances and eventually they lost sight of them.

"Well, I'd say we've been very lucky with our wildlife sightings," said Captain Gunn. "Didn't see a bear for Mark, but I'm just as glad not to, thank you very much! I can just see the headlines:

'English child devoured by grizzly bear in Canadian wilderness'! I'd have a hard time explaining that one to all your parents!"

AFTER SPENDING THE night in Pender Harbour, *South Islander* found its way into Buccaneer Bay on North Thormanby Island. The island boasted a beach almost as good as the ones on Savary, and the crew spent a couple of hours splashing and swimming in the warm water. It was beginning to feel like a summer holiday. Too bad it was almost over!

Captain Gunn wanted to have a look at Smuggler Cove just across from Buccaneer Bay on the Sunshine Coast.

"Wei Chen told me that smugglers used this cove before taking Chinese people over the border to the US," he said. "I'd like to have a look at it."

The entrance to the cove was narrow and led between a rocky bluff to port and some lower-lying rocks to starboard. Once inside, they were completely hidden from the channel outside, which was, of course, what had made it such a splendid hideout. They anchored in the first of several bays, and Captain Gunn took the dinghy with Ian rowing and Molly sitting in the bow with her bandaged arm. When they returned an hour later, Captain Gunn was in an extremely happy mood.

"This coast has so much history, and every time I turn around there's a new story begging to be written. I could stay here for years... Oh, don't worry," he added when he saw the look on Molly and Leticia's faces, "I've promised to be home for Christmas. That'll just give me enough time to finish my book on the Mounties and do some research on the next two I'm going to write. Don't forget I promised Jasper I'd write his story about his rum-running career, and of course, our friend Brother XII is going to make good reading."

That evening Sophie and Leticia really pulled out all the stops and produced a truly splendid dinner. There were sausages that had stayed fresh at the very bottom of the ice chest, a huge pot of potatoes mashed with masses of butter and milk, a tin of baked beans, and another of peas. Dessert was bananas and custard—an old standby and one of their favourites. And of course, at Mark's insistence they finished off with a double ration of chocolate.

"Phew, I'm glad the cooks are spared the washing up," groaned Leticia. "I can hardly move!"

Harriet was writing in her journal. "I've kept a record of every meal we've had. I bet you could write a book on boat cooking," she said to Sophie.

Thoughts turned to what they would be doing when they got back to England, but it was a gloomy thought considering the adventures they'd had and the wonderful cruise back to Vancouver they were now enjoying.

"Oh well," said Molly philosophically. "I suppose if this was all we did, the fun would wear off. We've really had the most splendid trip ever—I think we should give three cheers to Uncle Bert for arranging it."

As they were the only boat in the cove, they let loose with three splendid cheers for Captain Gunn, who sat modestly in his corner with his pipe and a small glass of whisky.

TWO DAYS LATER they were almost at the end of their voyage as they passed through the narrows into Burrard Inlet. Looking up, it was hard to imagine that soon a massive bridge would span the gap, suspended above the waters and carrying cars, lorries, and people from Stanley Park to West Vancouver.

"I think I'd much rather take a boat than risk crossing a bridge that's going to be so high," said Harriet.

"Suspension bridges are quite safe," replied Captain Gunn, "but really, they are a marvel of modern engineering. Imagine what the Romans would think of them. Those fellows were marvellous at building roads and aqueducts, but it took the Tibetans to come up with the first suspension bridge in about AD 1500. Took us Westerners about another three hundred years to figure them out, but they are used all over the world now and are a clever way of bridging places where it would be impractical to drive pilings."

As they rounded the end of Stanley Park and headed back to their dock in Coal Harbour, Leticia, who was stationed up on the foredeck, yelled back to the others in the cockpit: "There's a whole crowd of people standing on the dock by our spot. What can be going on?"

As they came in closer and Ian and Sophie got ready to jump ashore with the mooring lines, they recognized some faces in the crowd.

"Oh, look," said Harriet. "There's Joe Absolom and Jasper Peabody, and, golly, Jim Spilsbury's there too. Oh, and there's Pete the Mountie! How on earth did they know we were arriving today?"

As Ian and Sophie jumped smartly ashore and cleated the lines, the whole crew were astonished to hear the pop and see the flash of camera bulbs going off. It seemed that some of the crowd were reporters. There was even a man with a huge movie camera that had "Movietone News" emblazoned on its side. He was cranking a handle and shouting at the others to get out of the way.

"Well, I'll be darned," exclaimed Captain Gunn. "Looks like we're famous!"

Sergeant Pete and Jim Spilsbury pushed their way to the front of the crowd.

"I thought you'd make it back to Vancouver yesterday or today," said Jim. "There's been tremendous interest in Brother XII's gold and the gang of children that found it. The newspapers posted lookouts at Point Atkinson and they called in to their offices when you were spotted at the entrance to English Bay. I've been in contact with Joe and Jasper and told them to expect you—and here we all are to greet the returning heroes!"

The newspapermen were surging forwards with their notebooks and cameras, and the children all of sudden felt very shy about all the attention.

Pete turned and faced the crowd.

"All right, you lot, that's all you're going to get for today. We're going to set up a news conference in the next day or so, and you can ask all your questions then."

Gradually the crowd diminished until only those most connected with the crew of *South Islander* remained. One man whom they did not recognize remained. He was smartly dressed in a black suit and approached the edge of the dock.

"I'm Charles Shroeder, General Manager of the Hotel Vancouver, and I'd like to offer you a complimentary suite at the hotel for the duration of your stay in our fair city."

"That's very generous of you," replied Captain Gunn, "and timely too. We have to return *South Islander* to her owner tomorrow, and I was going to book us all into a hotel after that. We'd be delighted to take you up on your offer."

"If I might make a suggestion," continued Mr. Shroeder, "we could host the news conference in our ballroom."

As they were talking, another gentleman wearing a bowler hat and carrying a briefcase had approached the boat.

"Good day to you all," he said. "I see the news people found you. You're the most famous children in Canada right now! Oh, let me introduce myself. I'm Samuel Goldstein, and I've been representing the victims of Brother XII for the last couple of years. Not that there was much I could do for them until now. Anyway, once the officials have figured out the worth of the gold, my legal firm and I will be in charge of dispersing the money to the victims, and that will include handing over the reward for finding it. I'd be happy to handle the media attention for you, and we will have to meet to discuss business anyway before you leave Vancouver."

And so it was arranged. They would spend a last night on the boat and then pack their gear and move over to the hotel. The news conference would be scheduled for the next day.

Meanwhile, Captain Gunn had taken Jim Spilsbury aside and was chatting with him, out of earshot of the children.

The crew was talking to Joe and Jasper, and it was decided they would all meet at Wei Chen's restaurant that evening for dinner. It would be a happy occasion and would include Sergeant Pete and Jim Spilsbury in a great celebratory feast.

IT WAS WAY past their usual bedtime when they staggered back to the boat from their gargantuan dinner. Mr. Chen had produced a Chinese feast to beat all feasts with many specialities that weren't even on the menu. Captain Gunn declared it the best Chinese food he had ever tasted, and coming from a man who had travelled to the Far East and been to many places where a white face was a rarity and the food had no taint of Western influence, that was praise indeed.

Since it was their last night on *South Islander*, Sophie relaxed the bedtime rules further by allowing everyone to change into their pyjamas and sit up in the cockpit wrapped in blankets to enjoy a late-night chat.

"We need to be up early to pack, and I want to make sure that we leave the boat sparkling clean," said Sophie.

"I suppose we are going to need our 'pretties' for staying in the hotel," said Molly, referring to the detested party frocks that had spent the last couple of weeks languishing in the bottom of her duffel bag.

"I can't believe it's almost over," sighed Harriet. "What day do we have to catch the train back to Montreal?"

Captain Gunn was very vague about the impending return travel arrangements, so they left the subject and reminisced about their incredible adventures.

When the conversation finally slowed and the crew were stifling yawns, they all headed below for their last night on *South Islander*.

BY TEN O'CLOCK the next morning they were packed and ready to leave. Sophie had led a cleaning brigade and the boat had been scrubbed from stem to stern, including the ice box, stove, and all the woodwork down below. Up on deck, Ian and Captain Gunn had scrubbed the decks, furled and stowed all the sails under their neat green sail covers, and coiled every line on the boat. Mark had given the engine a thorough going over, checking the oil and leaving it ready to fire up and take the boat's owner on his next sailing trip. Even Posy was not spared. She had been given a rag soaked in lemon oil with which to polish the woodwork. Only Molly was excused from cleaning duties and, unused to inactivity, sat restless in the cockpit trying (unsuccessfully) to read a book.

When *South Islander* was deemed good enough to hand back to her owner, it was time to say goodbye. They had come to think of the boat as their own, and leaving her was like bidding farewell to an old friend. Leticia, Harriet, and Posy shed a few tears as they stepped off onto the dock for the last time. Mark's lip quivered as he did the same. Sophie and Ian were less emotional, but they too looked back longingly as they left the schooner behind. Molly was the last to make her exit, and she did it with her usual flair.

"Farewell, old girl," she said soulfully, patting the cabin roof as though it was a horse. "You served us well. We'll never forget you." Then she leapt onto the dock gracefully, even with her arm in a sling, and saluted *South Islander* like she was a Royal Navy captain instead of a pirate.

They borrowed a handcart and carried all their belongings up to the top of the dock. Captain Gunn had ordered a couple of taxis and they were whisked away from Coal Harbour and through downtown to the beautiful Hotel Vancouver.

They were met at the entrance by Mr. Schroeder, who personally escorted them to their rooms. They had been given two adjoining suites, each with two bedrooms, a splendidly gleaming bathroom with marble fixtures and an enormous clawfoot tub, and a living room equipped with a fireplace, easy chairs, and a large radio. Each suite had vases of fresh flowers scattered around, as well as a huge basket of fruit. Even Molly was struck dumb.

"Boys in one suite, girls in the other," said Sophie, taking charge as she always did in domestic arrangements. "I see they've put a rollaway bed in our suite, so Harriet and Posy will share one bedroom with me, and Molly and Leticia can have the other."

They discovered a connecting door between the suites, so with the door open they could call back and forth. The crew separated and got themselves unpacked.

"I'm going to ask Mr. Schroeder about laundry," said Sophie, "and I'll ask him at the same time about getting our good clothes ironed for the news conference."

The telephone in the boys' suite rang, and Captain Gunn answered it, speaking to whoever was at the other end for a couple of minutes.

"The news conference is at 2:00 this afternoon," he called through the adjoining door. "That was Mr. Goldstein, the lawyer. He's going to meet us downstairs at 1:45 and explain what's going to happen."

The reality of having to talk about their adventure to a crowd of press people was a little daunting to them all, but as Molly pointed out, if they could survive an earthquake, rushing rapids, and getting shot at, fielding a few questions would be a breeze.

Sophie ordered the crew to have a bath and change into clean clothes, and Mr. Schroeder had their newly ironed frocks and dress shorts delivered back to the suite in time for them all to present themselves in the girls' suite at 12:30 for inspection.

"I'd hardly recognize you lot as intrepid explorers and pirates," laughed Captain Gunn, who had kitted himself out in his version of dressing up—flannel trousers, a gaily striped shirt, a colourful scarf, and a very loud pair of suspenders. Not even a news conference could persuade him to put on socks and shoes; his feet were pushed into leather sandals as usual.

Molly grimaced and tugged at her flowered summer frock.

"I'm changing back as soon as this conference thing is over," she said, "and I don't think I'm going to need this sling much longer."

"Just wear it for the conference," said Captain Gunn. "Better if it doesn't look like you are entirely recovered—it'll make a more dramatic headline!"

Everyone headed down to the coffee shop for lunch (bottles of Coca Cola for everyone), and as they were finishing their meal Mr. Goldstein joined them.

"It's all arranged," he said. "We'll be having the press conference in the ballroom, and it's already half-full. We'll all sit at a table and they are setting up microphones so you can be heard at the back of the room."

Feeling a little nervous, the crew filed into the ballroom and seated themselves at the long table, facing a forest of microphones and a crowd wielding notebooks and cameras. The room quickly filled to bursting, and Mr. Goldstein rose to his feet, tapped the microphone to make sure it was working, and made his introductions.

"I'd like to introduce you to the daring and adventurous captain and crew of *South Islander*, who, relying on their wits and tenacity, were able to succeed where so many others have failed."

There was a huge burst of clapping and flash bulbs popping, and then the questions began, yelled from the floor and answered by various members of the crew through the microphones.

An hour later it was all over, and Captain Gunn and his fearless crew left through the back door, the crowd of reporters still shouting questions at them as they went.

"Phew, thank goodness that's over," said Leticia. "I'm not sure I like being famous!"

"Don't worry," said Captain Gunn, "the press are notoriously fickle. You'll be a seven-day wonder, and then something more interesting will happen and everyone will forget all about you!"

And with that sobering thought, the crew changed back into their comfortable clothes and headed out to take in the sights of Vancouver.

CHAPTER FOURTEEN

GOODBYE TO THE WEST COAST

THE NEXT MORNING, before heading down to breakfast, the crew found a pile of newspapers outside their doors. They were front-page news! The whole story of finding the treasure, accompanied by photographs of them, was sprawled across the front page of every newspaper. Quotes and misquotes abounded, but mostly they got the story right and it seemed a lot of people were very happy with the results of their treasure hunt.

They went downstairs and enjoyed a Canadian breakfast of bacon, waffles, and maple syrup in the hotel's coffee shop.

"I'm going to take some maple syrup back home with me," said Mark through a mouthful of waffle.

"I'm not sure you're going to have room in your duffel bag for maple syrup as well as the jars of peanut butter you want to take," laughed Leticia.

"Well, if I don't have room, the rest of you can put some in your luggage. After all, you're going to get a share of it all when we get home," said Mark, eyeing those crewmembers who had shown a similar passion for peanut butter and maple syrup.

The day before, they had taken the ferry from Coal Harbour over to North Vancouver and then caught a bus up the winding road to the Capilano Suspension Bridge. The bridge hung high over the Capilano River, and crossing it took a lot of courage. Leticia admitted that in addition to being terrified of thunder she wasn't too keen on heights, but when she saw the younger members of the crew skip fearlessly over the bridge, she swallowed her fear and made the crossing.

After tea in the teahouse beside the bridge, they made their way back over Burrard Inlet and then to the zoo in Stanley Park. Mark made a beeline for the bear exhibit, and stood staring through the bars at a sad-looking pair of grizzly bears.

"Just as well we didn't meet them in the wild," he said. "They're awfully big and don't look too friendly."

"I don't think you'd feel too friendly if you were stuck in a horrid cage year after year being gawked at by tourists," laughed Molly. "Come on, let's go and have a look at the wolves."

AS THEY SAT in the coffee shop enjoying their waffles the next morning, talk turned to the upcoming journey home.

"When do we catch the train, Uncle Bert?" asked Leticia.

Just as Captain Gunn was opening his mouth to reply, they caught sight of Jim Spilsbury walking towards them.

"Ah, Jim. Just in time," said Captain Gunn, relieved. "I don't think I could hold off the questions from this inquisitive lot much longer."

"It's all fixed," said Jim.

"What's fixed?" asked Molly.

"Well, now, your friend Jim here has been kind enough to arrange an alternate form of transportation for your trip back to Montreal. I thought the train company did such a good job of getting you here, we shouldn't trust our luck in getting you all back safely. Not with Mark here wanting to drive the train and Molly being a target of armed train robbers!"

"What on earth are you talking about?" said Molly.

"Jim here has a surprise for you," beamed Captain Gunn.

"Your uncle asked me to find out if it would be possible to fly you back to Montreal instead of taking the train," began Jim. "I called in a few favours, and I think we have lift-off! A friend of mine owns a small airline, Canadian Airways. He's just bought a brand spanking new airplane—a Junkers Ju 52. He's doing an inaugural flight with it across Canada to advertise his freight services, and taking you along will make marvellous publicity. As long as you don't mind getting your photos taken at every stop, you all have a free ride to Montreal. He's based in Winnipeg, but he's bringing a load of mining equipment to Vancouver that I'm going to deliver up North, and as part of his publicity flight he's taking cases of west coast salmon to deliver at all his stops. I believe he's delivering shipments to Calgary, Winnipeg, and Thunder Bay before making a grand arrival in Montreal."

It took a moment for the news to sink in. The crewmembers looked at each other in disbelief. Finally, Molly spoke up.

"Thank you so much," she said, with uncharacteristic composure. "It will be the most perfect end to our adventures."

The others looked at her in astonishment. Molly overwhelmed was a very strange sight indeed.

"I'll need you to be at the aerodrome at 6:00 a.m. tomorrow," said Jim. "The whole trip is going to take about twenty hours with the stops. The press will be at every stop, but we'll try to limit them to a quick photo of you, the famous passengers, and a comment or two from my friend about his new air service. By the way, his name is James Richardson, and I've known him since we were kids. He's a few years older than me, but we've flown together a lot. You won't find a better pilot—except me, of course—in all of western Canada."

THAT EVENING THE hotel hosted a farewell dinner for the crew. Invited were all their old friends, as well as some of the former victims of Brother xii who had been contacted by Mr. Goldstein. Some of them were glad to accept the invitation and meet the children who had found their money, but others were shy and ashamed of the fact that they had been taken in by such a rogue.

The detested "pretties" were brought out again, and Sophie insisted the girls wear their very best white party frocks with white socks, patent leather shoes, and hair ribbons that matched the sashes on their frocks. Molly rebelled at the hair ribbons and declared that she, the fearless pirate, would come wearing her red cap. Sophie gave in. The boys were dressed in flannel shorts, white shirts and ties, knee socks, and polished lace-up shoes. The less said about Captain Gunn's outfit the better, but he did his best and looked slightly more reputable than usual.

The ballroom had been set up with two long tables and another across the top where the crew would sit. The tables were set with fine china emblazoned with the hotel's emblem, crystal glasses, and gleaming silverware. Down each table were arrangements of flowers. It all looked rather like a wedding reception. The children felt slightly shy at all the attention and fuss that was being made of them, but were soon put at ease by seeing their old friends dressed in their Sunday best.

Joe Absolom was there, as well as Jasper the rum-runner, Pete the Mountie in his red dress uniform, and Jim Spilsbury. Mr. Goldstein was there chatting to some people the children did not know but whom they assumed were other Brother XII victims.

Mr. Schroeder, the manager of the hotel, asked everyone to be seated and then handed over to Mr. Goldstein, who gave a speech that made the children blush. He waxed poetic about how if all children were as brave, adventurous, and steadfast in the face of danger as the crew of *South Islander*, the world would be a better place.

Eventually the speech making ended and the party settled down to a truly splendid dinner. At the end, a large cake in the shape of a treasure chest was wheeled in and glasses of champagne were raised in toasts. (Even the children were allowed a small taste.) The evening wrapped up with everyone mingling and hearing at first hand about some of the crew's adventures during their treasure-hunting cruise.

As they had an early start the next morning, Sophie hustled them all off to bed at a reasonable hour, and as they left the ballroom the guests raised a rousing cheer. It was a most wonderful end to their stay in Vancouver.

EARLY THE NEXT morning they bid farewell, with many thanks for his hospitality, to Mr. Schroeder and were taken in two taxis out to the aerodrome on Sea Island, outside Vancouver. As they pulled up to the wooden terminal building, they saw a gleaming silver plane sitting on the apron way. It had "Canadian Airways" emblazoned on the side, and there was a lorry pulled up to the open cargo door to load cases of tinned salmon onto the plane.

During their quick breakfast that morning before leaving the hotel, they had suddenly realized that they would also be saying goodbye to Captain Gunn, at least for the time being. He told them that he would be spending the next couple of months in Vancouver doing research for his upcoming books.

"I've booked a small apartment in the Sylvia Hotel," he had said. "It's a lovely place, right down on English Bay. I have a view of the water and can watch the boats going into False Creek. It will be very restful without you lot dragging me off on adventures, and I shall spend a lot of time in the city library. Don't worry, I'm booked on a ship that will get me back to England early in December, and I'm hoping we will all meet in Scotland over the Christmas holidays."

Now, standing beside the airplane, the moment of parting arrived. His nephew and nieces flung themselves into his arms, and even Molly shed a tear or two. As everyone said their goodbyes, two men climbed down out of the plane. One was Jim Spilsbury, the other an older man. Jim introduced them to James Richardson, the owner of the airline and pilot on this cross-Canada flight, who greeted them cordially and helped them all to board. A couple of reporters had obviously got wind of their departure, and photographs were taken of the departing heroes.

Soon the seven adventurers were strapped into their seats in front of the cases of salmon, and the plane sped down the runway, lifting into the air over the waters of Georgia Strait. The children craned their necks to see the beautiful vista of city, park, and mountains as the plane swung around in a circle and headed east to its first stop in Calgary.

TWENTY-TWO HOURS LATER, at 4:00 the next morning, the plane landed in Montreal. They had been greeted in Calgary, Winnipeg, and Thunder Bay by crowds of reporters and had had their photos taken dozens of times. It was really fantastic publicity for Mr. Richardson's airline. The children's faces—set against the backdrop of the airplane with a smiling Mr. Richardson standing to one side—would be plastered all over newspapers from coast to coast.

During the flight, he invited them to take turns sitting in the third seat up in the cockpit. Molly spent the longest time there, asking all sorts of questions through her headphones. She was completely smitten with the experience of flying and ended the flight even more determined to earn her pilot's licence as soon as possible.

Jim Spilsbury's aunt who lived in Montreal met them at the airport. They would stay the remainder of the night with her and she would put them on the train to Quebec City in the morning.

"We've arranged for a steward off the ship to meet you at the train station and help you and your luggage to the docks where you'll board the ship," she said as she showed a very tired crew to their rooms. "You'll be glad to get on-board ship and get away from all this fuss. You must be exhausted."

And they were. It had been a very long day, and they would only get a few hours' sleep before being rushed off to the train station. Posy had been carried off the plane fast asleep and had not woken up during the short journey to Jim's aunt's house, but the others had managed to stay awake for most of the flight. They dropped into their beds without so much as brushing their teeth and were soon fast asleep.

The next day they did the whole journey from Montreal to Quebec in reverse, and by late afternoon they were once again climbing the gangplank onto the *Empress of Britain*. It felt a little like coming home.

IT WAS A relaxing trip back across the Atlantic. Their fame had preceded them, and they were again invited to dine at the captain's table, but there were no reporters and they were mostly left to their own devices. Harriet reacquainted herself with the librarian, who was thrilled to hear that the idea that had originated in her library had turned into such an incredible adventure. Mark sought out Bill from the engine room, Ian spent a lot of time on the bridge, and the rest of them played games, read, and enjoyed the plentiful and delicious meals.

Five days later the great ocean liner was nudged into her dock by a bevy of busy tugs. As soon as the gangplank had been secured, the children were the first to disembark and were met on the dock by their mothers, who were laughing and crying at the same time.

"Molly, how could you go and get yourself shot?" exclaimed her mother, looking her over and noticing that there was only a small bandage left over the wound. She had been forewarned about her daughter's injury by a long telegram from her brother.

"Well, I'm glad I did," replied Molly indignantly. "If I hadn't, those villains would probably have got off lightly and would still be out there bothering innocent people."

Mrs. MacTavish was heading back to Scotland with her three children, and Mrs. Phillips was taking her four off-spring back to their home in Devon, where they would have some time to regale their mother with all the stories of their adventures. Ian was due to start at the naval college in a few weeks, and the girls would be heading back to their board-ing school in Wales. Real life was taking over from the almost unbelievable adventures they had experienced. It was a sober-ing thought.

They travelled back to London together and then planned on going their separate ways. Trains to Scotland and the north of England departed from a different station to those heading west to Devon, so once the train from Southampton arrived at Waterloo Station it was time to part company.

The goodbyes between the two groups of crewmembers were hard, but Mrs. MacTavish reminded them that they would be reunited a few months later at their home in Scotland.

"Don't look so glum—you'll all be grown up and leaving school far too soon, and then you'll look back on your school days and wish you were back there!"

It really was the end of an epic adventure—one they would remember for the rest of their lives. The idea of making their cruise a treasure hunt had been a good one, but even Harriet, who had come up with the idea, could never have imagined where the trail would lead them and the incredible adventures they would have along the way. Even though this particular adventure was now over, they all knew that there would be many more to come. It was time to leave the past behind them and look forward.

EPILOGUE

Christmas 1936

THE WIND RATTLED against the panes of the big living room at An Cuileann, but inside it was warm with a large wood fire crackling in the hearth. It was a big party—the four Phillips children with both their parents and the three MacTavishes with their mother and uncle. They had just finished a gargantuan Christmas dinner, prepared by Mrs. Baird, the cook (that doughty lady who knew exactly the tastes of explorers and pirates), assisted by Sophie (who had to admit she enjoyed cooking from time to time—as long as she didn't miss out on any adventures in the process), and the two mothers. The adults were dozing, and the children were reminiscing about the adventures of the past summer.

"I wonder how Joe is doing," said Harriet.

Captain Gunn sat up abruptly.

"I almost forgot—I've got a letter here from Mr. Goldstein."

Molly pounced on him. "'Almost forgot!' Honestly, Uncle Bert. Anyone would think you were getting old!"

Captain Gunn was rummaging in the pockets of his jacket and finally came up with a letter bearing a Canadian stamp. He found his reading glasses in another pocket, pulled out several sheets of paper, spread them out, and began to read.

Dear Mr. Cameron,

Since you left Vancouver last month, there have been some significant developments in the case of the recovered gold and reward pertaining to it.

Once the police and the various government departments had decided whom the money belonged to, it was passed on to me in trust for the victims of Brother xii. It will be divided up depending on how much money those victims "invested" with Brother xii.

However, before all expenses relating to the case have been settled and the money is divided between the victims, there is the matter of the reward. There did not seem to be any precedent for assigning a reward in such a case—no one has recovered treasure of this sort in living memory. After much discussion between the various parties involved, it was decided that 10 percent of the value of the gold should go to the captain and crew of *South Islander*.

The value of the treasure, once it was converted from gold coin into Canadian dollars, was $183,568.23. The reward was calculated on the total value, before any other expenses were paid and thus the amount that will be disbursed to you and your crew is $18,356.82. That money will be wired to your bank for you to divide into eight, one share for you, seven for your crew.

On a related matter, Joe Absolom, whom I believe you first met on De Courcy Island, has asked me to pass on to you his very best wishes. He is not much of a letter writer but would like you to know what he will be doing with his share of the money.

He is in the process of buying a house in Nanaimo, where he can be close to his wife who is currently residing in the mental hospital. Apparently Maggie is doing much better, has begun to speak again, and is now going out on day passes with Joe. Although she will never totally recover, Joe is hopeful that she will be able to return to live at home and live a fairly normal life.

I trust that you will find the arrangements regarding the reward to your satisfaction. It was with the greatest pleasure that I made the acquaintance of you and your intrepid crew. They are excellent role models for other young people, and I am quite sure will all go on to do extraordinary things as adults.

Yours very sincerely,
SAMUEL GOLDSTEIN

POSTSCRIPT

Each of the eight members of the crew of *South Islander* received $2,294. Here is what they did with the money:

- Captain Gunn's share went into "general revenue," meaning that he put it towards further foreign travel. He also had double-glazed windows installed at An Cuileann, which cut down on the whistling draughts it had previously been subject to during the long Scottish winters.
- Ian bought a fourteen-foot sailing dinghy to use when on leave from naval college.
- Sophie put hers in a savings account for post-secondary education. She plans to go to cooking school in Switzerland after she finishes boarding school and wants to become a world-famous chef. She hopes her dishes will be admired and written up in gourmet magazines—and never, ever taken for granted!
- Harriet put hers in a savings account to pay for a course in French history at the Sorbonne in Paris.
- Mark bought a very superior train set, put the rest into savings. He plans to be an engineer when he leaves school.

- Leticia decided she didn't need anything that money could buy and donated hers to an orphanage in China.
- Posy's share was put into a savings account until she was old enough to decide what she wanted to do with it.
- And last but definitely not least, Molly has hers earmarked for flying lessons next summer. She fully intends to be a Canadian bush pilot.

GLOSSARY OF NAUTICAL TERMS

ANCHOR RODE A chain or rope attached to the anchor.

BEAM REACH A point of sail where the wind is blowing at right angles to the boat.

BOOM A SPAR at the bottom of the main sail.

BOW The front or pointy end of the boat.

BOWSPRIT A SPAR extending from the bow over the water.

BROAD REACH A point of sailing in which the wind blows over a boat's quarter, between the beam and the stern.

BULWARKS The raised edge of the deck, which runs all the way round the boat.

CHART The nautical equivalent of a map.

CLINKER-BUILT A boat built with overlapping planks rather than planks joined edge to edge.

CLOSE HAULED Having the sails set for sailing as nearly against the wind as the vessel will go—usually around thirty degrees off the wind.

COCKPIT The place from which the boat is steered and passengers sit, usually located near the STERN of the boat.

COMPANIONWAY Stairs leading down below deck.

DAVITS A hoist that is sometimes used to raise the DINGHY to store it on deck.

DINGHY A small boat usually towed astern, used for going ashore from anchor.

DRAFT OF A BOAT How much the boat measures from the waterline to the bottom of the KEEL.

FATHOM One fathom equals six feet.

FORESAIL On a SCHOONER, the sail rigged between the two masts.

GALLEY A boat or ship's kitchen.

GAFF-RIGGED A boat that has a SPAR at the top of the mainsail, making the sail four-sided.

GUNWALE The top rail of the BULWARK.

GYBING To shift a fore-and-aft sail from one side of a vessel to the other while sailing before the wind so as to sail on the opposite tack.

HALYARDS The ropes used to raise and lower the sails.

HEAD The bathroom on a boat.

HEAVE-TO Coming to a stop while sailing by turning across the wind, leaving the headsail backed. A power vessel would turn into the seas and apply just enough power to maintain position.

JIB A smaller sail rigged at the front of the boat.

KEEL The bit under the boat that gives it stability in the water.

KNOT A unit of speed. One knot equals one NAUTICAL MILE per hour.

LEAD LINE A length of line for swinging a lead, marked at various points to indicate multiples of fathoms. Used to measure depth.

MAINSAIL Usually the largest of the sails.

NAUTICAL MILE One nautical mile equals approximately 1.8 kilometres.

PORT The left side.

RUNNING Sailing with the wind almost directly behind the boat.

SALOON The living room on a boat.

SCHOONER A type of boat with two masts, the shorter one being towards the BOW.

SHEETS The ropes used to control the sails.

SPARS The rigid bits that support the sails.

STARBOARD The right side.

STAYSAIL Another FORESAIL, larger than the JIB and rigged forward of the foremast.

STERN The back of the boat.

TACKING Changing course by turning a boat's head into and through the wind while sailing close hauled. A boat can be on the port or the starboard tack depending on which direction the wind is coming from.

ACKNOWLEDGEMENTS

TO LARA KORDIC at Heritage House, who saw the potential in this book.

To the English public (private) school system, which, despite its many deficiencies, did teach me to sew, cook, and, most importantly, type and write grammatically correct English.

To my dear friend Molly March, who has been along with me on my publishing journey since 2009 and who spent countless hours on the exquisite artwork in this book.

And finally, to my wonderful husband, who, even while building an airplane and running a business, always took the time to listen to passages from the book, and who allowed me to read the finished manuscript to him. He had many useful comments and suggestions, some of which I even used!

ABOUT THE AUTHOR

After a childhood spent in England, where she attended boarding school and teacher training college, AMANDA SPOTTISWOODE immigrated to Canada in the 1970s and settled on Salt Spring Island in 1995. In 1997 she co-founded Graffiti Theatre Company, which she ran for fifteen years before retiring in 2012.

Adam Gilmer, Lightwell Photography

As a child, Amanda was taught to sail by the Royal Navy on the River Thames. After moving to Salt Spring, she finally realized her childhood dream of sailing and exploring a rugged coastline by boat. Amanda and her husband, Tom Navratil, have spent every summer since 1998 cruising on their thirty-four-foot wooden sloop, *South Islander*, exploring the waters between the Southern Gulf Islands and the north end of Vancouver Island. These travels were the inspiration for her first book, *South Islander: Memoirs of a Cruising Dog* (2013).

8005

Amanda has two children—a daughter who lives in Geneva with her husband, and a son who is a professional photographer and lives with his wife in Victoria—and one grandchild.

ARTIST, SET DESIGNER, and travel- ler, MOLLY MARCH has painted and designed the- atre sets for operas, ballets, and plays all over the world—from Hawaii to London and from British Colum- bia to Chile. She has been creating shows with BC theatre companies Runaway Moon Theatre, Caravan Farm Theatre, and Leaky Heaven Circus for the past thirty years. Molly illustrated Amanda Spottiswoode's first book, *South Islander: Memoirs of a Cruising Dog*, creating the artwork for the thirty-one charming maps included in the book. She lives in Coldstream, BC.